"You can tell me," Isaac said.

Daniella pulled away. "Tell you what?"

"Why you're so afraid."

He thought she was going to leave the hospital room without replying, but then she said, "I just hate bombs, that's all. They're so indiscriminate. So lethal."

Isaac nodded. "This one wasn't much, if that helps any."

The heartrending look in her emerald-green eyes penetrated his defenses despite his strong resolve. It had been a long time since he'd seen that much poignancy and sorrow in a person's gaze.

This shy, quiet woman had given his heart a twist without saying a word.

Why is she so afraid?

* * *

CAPITOL K-9 UNIT:
These lawmen solve the toughest cases
with the help of their brave canine partners

Valerie Hansen was thirty when she awoke to the presence of the Lord in her life and turned to Jesus. She now lives in a renovated farmhouse in the breathtakingly beautiful Ozark mountains of Arkansas and is privileged to share her personal faith by telling the stories of her heart for Love Inspired. Life doesn't get much better than that!

Books by Valerie Hansen

Love Inspired Suspense

Capitol K-9 Unit

Detecting Danger

The Defenders

Nightwatch
Threat of Darkness
Standing Guard
A Trace of Memory

Serenity, Arkansas

Her Brother's Keeper
Out of the Depths
Shadow of Turning
Nowhere to Run
No Alibi
My Deadly Valentine
"Dangerous Admirer"

Visit the Author Profile page at Harlequin.com for more titles.

DETECTING DANGER

VALERIE HANSEN

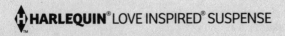

HARLEQUIN® LOVE INSPIRED® SUSPENSE

Special thanks and acknowledgment are given to Valerie Hansen for her contribution to the Capitol K-9 Unit miniseries

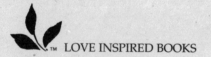

Recycling programs
for this product may
not exist in your area.

LOVE INSPIRED BOOKS

ISBN-13: 978-0-373-44678-0

Detecting Danger

www.Harlequin.com

Printed in U.S.A.

Fear not for I am with you; be not dismayed for I am your God.
I will strengthen you, yes, I will help you.
I will uphold you with My righteous right hand.
—*Isaiah* 41:10

To my Joe, who is with me in spirit, looking over my shoulder and offering moral support as I write. He always will be.

ONE

"Capitol K-9 Unit Five, safety check at Washington Monument complete," Isaac Black radioed via the com-link he wore. "DC police are also on scene for crowd control."

"Copy," echoed back into his earpiece. "Stand by."

Isaac turned his attention to Detective David Delvecchio of the DC Metro squad and smiled. "You look like something's bugging you. What's the matter?"

"I'm just not fond of congressmen who throw their weight around and cause unnecessary overtime." He eyed the gaggle of news vans and cameramen surrounding Harland Jeffries. "If he wants to grandstand he should do it on his own turf."

"And preferably during office hours," Isaac added. He glanced down at Abby, his brown-and-white bomb-detecting beagle. She had stretched out on the grassy verge skirting the Washington Monument, panting and cooling off after the excitement of doing her job. "At least one of us is happy to be working tonight."

"Yeah. I'm sure glad we have you and the rest of the K-9 team on call. My men didn't have time to do a proper sweep of this area. By the time we got the word about the congressman's impromptu press conference, we only had an hour to deploy."

Isaac nodded. "Not to worry. If Abby says there's no bomb on the grounds, it's safe. You can trust her."

"I do," Delvecchio replied.

Curious tourists were gathering outside the police line, milling around and straining to get a peek at whoever was the center of attention. Politicians and their aides in dark business suits stood out against the colorful garb of the bystanders as Secret Service agents would have at a three-ring circus performance.

Isaac was about to withdraw to his SUV and wait to be released when he noticed his dog stiffen and ease to her feet. Since he had not given the command, her independent actions drew his attention.

"Abby?" He crouched, following the beagle's line of sight. She was clearly focused on the small group nearest to the congressman. "What is it, girl?"

Instead of relaxing, the dog froze in place, her hackles bristling. Her nose quivered. Her tail was half-raised and still. If they had not just completed a search of the premises Isaac would think...

He stood and grabbed the detective's sleeve. "Pull everybody back. Clear the area. Now!" Isaac's commanding tone left no doubt of his seriousness.

"Why? What do you see?"

"Nothing," Isaac said. "But Abby senses something's wrong and that's good enough for me."

Delvecchio was already shouting into his radio. Patrol officers immediately began to shoo bystanders farther away from the monument.

Isaac moved forward with Abby. "Seek it, girl. Seek it."

They didn't have far to go. The little beagle cut straight across the inner circle, zeroed in on a briefcase leaning against the base of one of the concrete benches that ringed the obelisk and plunked down into a sit.

"I have a suspicious object on the west side, at about two o'clock from the police staging area," Isaac reported via the com-link.

His new orders followed in moments. "Secure the area and pull back to a safe distance. Bomb squad is on its way."

"Copy."

He scooped up his dog, checked to make sure no one else remained nearby and would be in danger, then began to jog away.

As he ran, time seemed to slow unnaturally. His feet weighed a ton, making him feel as if he were slogging through cold molasses.

Tension grew with every step, pressing against him and making his heart pound.

Abby was trembling as though she sensed impending doom.

Suddenly, a concussion rocked the atmosphere. Isaac saw the flash through his closed eyelids an instant before he heard the blast.

Instinct made him hunch over his dog's body to protect her as he was knocked to his knees by the force of the explosion.

Most of the debris it created fell like fistfuls of tossed pebbles, but a few chunks of concrete were heavy enough, large and jagged enough, to do damage.

One piece grazed his shoulder. Another hit the back of his lower leg. Both stunned him rather than caused immediate pain.

How could this have happened? Abby is never wrong.

Which meant that the bomb had to have been placed there *after* he and the dog had made their rounds. That fact should narrow the list of suspects considerably.

Propping himself on one elbow with the other arm gripping his wiggling partner, Isaac tried to blink the grit from his watering eyes. Gray, cloudy residue filled the air. People coughed and wheezed. Many were in full flight while a few others had paused with cell phones to take macabre pictures of the chaos.

Isaac rolled into a sitting position and brushed himself off. He first checked to make sure Abby was all right, then peered back toward the source of the blast to check for casualties.

"Please, God," he prayed, "let my warning have been in time."

He rubbed his smarting eyes on the sleeve of his uniform jacket. It looked as if there were some injuries but the apparent victims were all on their feet. A few were reeling and being assisted by police and friends. Others appeared merely stunned. A cacophony of horns and sirens filled the night.

Ears ringing, head spinning, Isaac knew what he must do. There was no time to waste. Where there was one bomb there could easily be another. And another.

He wanted to lie back on the cool grass, close his eyes and wait for full recovery of his senses, but that was not how he and his fellow K-9 officers operated. The public came first. He'd tend his wounds later. As long as Abby was all right, they'd keep doing their job.

Isaac tightened up on the leash, struggled to his feet and took a step forward. His calf muscles knotted.

Intense pain radiated from his boot to his hip and dropped him where he stood.

The flow of patients through the ER at DC General Hospital had been surprisingly sparse for a balmy spring evening. Daniella Dunne stifled a yawn and smiled at a fellow RN who was also battling to stay alert.

"Every time we have a slow night I wonder why I like this shift so much," Daniella remarked.

"Because you crave adrenaline just like the rest of us," the older woman replied. "When this place starts to really hop we all feel a lot more alive."

"I suppose you're right." As far as Daniella was concerned, staying awake half the night was profoundly better than working days when so many more reporters and photographers were liable to be on the job. The last thing she needed was to become an unwilling star of some viral video. She'd matured and changed her hair color from blond to brunette, long to shorter, but that didn't mean she wouldn't be recognized by the same criminal element that had caused her to enter witness protection in the first place.

"Prepare for casualties," someone shouted. "There's just been an incident at the Washington Monument!"

Daniella froze for a heartbeat, then jumped to her feet and hurried down the hallway to the ambulance receiving area, where the majority of the night shift was gathering around a police scanner.

"Was it an accident?" one of the young orderlies asked.

"Doesn't sound like it. The first responders pegged it as a bomb," someone else answered.

Daniella clenched her fists. Her stomach churned. She suddenly saw herself as a frightened teenager again and pictured her father being arrested for the bombing death of her mother. Ten long years had passed since then, yet those terrible memories were as vivid as if everything had just happened.

Her initial disbelief about her mother's fate had quickly been supplanted with righteous anger, especially when she'd heard her estranged father begin to laugh. *Laugh!* And so she had done the only thing she could. She had mustered her courage and agreed to testify against him in court.

While most of the ER staff remained gathered around the scanner, Daniella eased away and headed for the hospital chapel.

Until the victims of this current attack arrived for treatment, the best thing she could do was pray. Fervently. The way she had prayed for her mother—even though she'd known in her deepest heart that Mama's survival was impossible.

Being incapacitated made Isaac frustrated and angry. He'd repeatedly waved off paramedics, sending them to tend to others. As the area was systematically cleared, however, he realized he was eventually going to have to let the medics look at his throbbing leg.

Detective Delvecchio approached. "I wondered where you'd gotten to. Is Abby all right?"

"Yes." Isaac tried to rise and was stopped by the other man's hand on his shoulder. "Relax, man."

"I can't. There's work to do. What if there's a second bomb?"

"If there is, your team will find it. Some of them are sweeping the area now. So far, so good."

Isaac heaved a sigh. "Thank God—literally."

"I have been. Particularly since there don't seem to be any life-threatening injuries."

"That's a relief."

"Yeah, and a surprise. So, are you ready to go to the hospital?"

The detective offered a hand and Isaac took it, grimacing as he rose. Standing wasn't too painful as long as he kept weight off his injured leg by leaning on David's shoulder.

"If you can make it to my car I'll drive you to the ER."

"That's against protocol."

"Your choice," Delvecchio said, arching a brow. "All the ambulances are busy. I consider this an extenuating circumstance, but it's up to you. Do you want to wait?"

"No." Isaac leaned slightly to glance at his calf. Blood had stuck the dark fabric of his uniform to his lower leg but seemed to have stopped flowing for the present.

"Why don't you help me to my car so I don't get yours dirty?"

"That's what plastic sheets are for," the detective said with a slight smile. "There's no way I'm letting you drive in your condition. I saw you send the medics to other victims and I figured it was high time you got some TLC yourself."

Isaac managed a smile. "No offense, buddy, but I'd rather have a pretty nurse taking care of me than a bossy cop like you."

Chuckling, Delvecchio slipped his arm around Isaac's waist for added support and started to move toward his unmarked car. "I'll see what I can do about finding the right nurse when we get to the hospital. What about Abby?"

"I'll handle my dog. You just get me to a doctor who can sew me up so I can go back to work."

"You're pushing it again."

Isaac sobered, glancing over his shoulder. "I know. But I feel responsible for what happened tonight and I intend to catch whoever did this."

"I've already ordered every news crew to give me copies of their raw footage. My men are also collecting the shots taken by bystanders so we can run facial recognition on anyone we don't know."

Pausing, Isaac gave the man a serious look. "Don't just concentrate on strangers. Watch the politicians, too, particularly Harland Jeffries and his staff. Considering his long-standing reputation in dirty politics, I wouldn't put it past him to try to create sympathy by pretending to be exposed to possible injury. It wouldn't be the first lie he'd ever told."

Isaac got a sinking feeling when David shook his head. "I strongly doubt that's what took place tonight," the detective said.

"Why? Was he hurt in the blast?"

"No. He may be a master manipulator but he was complaining of chest pains when they hauled him away. If this bomb scare was supposed to boost his chances of getting his new crime bill passed and it caused him to have a heart attack instead, he badly miscalculated."

Daniella had been working behind the scenes while one of the on-call doctors did triage on the victims. None seemed badly hurt and outside of a little first aid, a few stitches and a tranquilizer here and there, they had been easy to treat.

She was cleaning up one of the exam cubicles and hoping she could avoid the reporters who were still milling around the lobby when the head nurse separated a gap in the heavy curtains.

"I've got another victim here—brought in by private vehicle. All the doctors are busy and we're out of wheelchairs. Take care of him for me, will you?"

"Of course."

Daniella relieved the other nurse and slipped her arm around the uniformed officer's waist, starting to guide him. She was careful to avert her face for the brief moments when she was exposed to the public, hoping no cameras would capture her image. That was when she noted the leash in the patient's hand. "I'm terribly sorry. You can't bring a dog into the hospital."

"This isn't a dog."

"Sure looks like one."

"Nope. This is officer Abby of the Capitol K-9 Unit. See her vest?"

"She's still a dog."

"I beg to differ. You permit service dogs, don't you?"

"Yes, of course, but…"

"Then you have to allow Abby in. Besides, I'm injured and she's my partner. She goes where I go."

"Do you promise to take the flak if the hospital administration finds out and pitches a fit?"

"No problem. I'm already wearing a flak vest under my jacket." He glanced toward the foyer, where Delvecchio was speaking to additional reporters. "Don't I have to fill out paperwork?"

The direct answer was yes. Daniella chose to handle it another way in order to keep her distance from the news crews. "I can help you with those details while you hold your dog—I mean your partner."

She helped him lie down and lifted his boots to rest on the narrow exam table. When she picked up a PDA and began poking its screen with a stylus, she wished her hands would stop shaking. "Your name, please?"

"Isaac Black. How long have you worked in ER?" he asked, frowning.

When his fascinating, dark gaze locked with her green eyes she could barely force herself to look away. "Seven years. Why?"

"Because you're acting awfully nervous. You aren't afraid of dogs, are you?"

"Don't be silly. I love animals."

"Then what's wrong? If you had already examined my leg I'd think I was hurt worse than I'd imagined."

"I'm sure you'll be fine, Mr.—I mean Officer— Black."

"May as well call me Isaac. It solves lots of problems."

"Fine. Can you put the dog on a chair long enough for you to be treated?"

"Of course. If I'd been able to drive myself over here I'd have left her at headquarters. Unfortunately, I was overruled."

"A wise decision," Daniella said. She laid the tablet aside while her patient pointed to a chair and the beagle obediently jumped into it.

"I'm impressed," she said. "My cat barely comes when I call him for supper."

"Not surprising. Cats have devious minds."

If he hadn't been smiling at her, Daniella might have thought he was serious. "That's debatable."

The resulting twinkle in his dark eyes was so appealing she had to force herself to look away. He was taller than most of the men she knew, and far more muscular. His smile was amiable enough, yet there was an aura about him that made her think of danger. Either that or she was simply being influenced by the disquieting thoughts that had begun the moment she'd heard the news of an explosion.

Once she had recorded Isaac's necessary preliminary information, she slit the leg of his uniform pants the rest of the way to his knee, folded back the fabric and carefully removed his boot.

"Well? How bad is it?" he asked.

"The doctor will make that assessment when he gets here."

"Let me put it this way." Isaac reached for her wrist and clasped it, gently but firmly, sending another shiver zinging up her spine. "If I just bandage it up and go back to work, will I be sorry?"

"I would certainly think so."

He heaved a telling sigh. "That's what I was afraid of."

"You got hurt at the monument, like the others, right?"

"Right. Abby and I were there to do a safety inspection of the area. She couldn't have missed detecting the bomb. It had to be placed there *after* we made our sweep. There's no other possible explanation."

Her brain absorbed very little more after he said *bomb*. That word had been a trigger for a surge of negative emotions for many years, and this instance was no different. Latent fear gripped her heart, stilled her movements and turned her fingers to stone. It wasn't until she felt his warm touch on her forearm that she snapped out of it. Sort of.

"You okay?" The dark, dancing eyes had narrowed and he was studying her as if she were a specimen under a microscope.

"I'm fine."

"You keep telling me that but every now and then I see something else."

"Must be your imagination," Daniella assured him.

The expression on the police officer's face was clear. He didn't believe her. And little wonder since she was anything but fine. Matter of fact, at this moment, all she wanted to do was run out the door, disappear into the night, leave everything behind and never look back.

TWO

Isaac had been visited by a physician and was sporting twenty-three stitches by the time his boss, Captain Gavin McCord, arrived at the hospital and began berating him.

"You broke at least two rules tonight. You should have cleared that area the instant your dog alerted and waited for an ambulance instead of hitching a ride," McCord said with a scowl. "Care to tell me what happened?"

"I did clear it. The problem wasn't because of me or Abby." Isaac had been enjoying the pretty nurse's company as she'd begun to bandage his calf and he smiled in her direction.

McCord eyed her, too. "Could you finish that later? I'd like to talk to my team member privately."

"Of course." She stripped off her latex gloves.

In spite of her quick, compliant reply, Isaac could tell she was hesitant to leave him. Why? They hardly knew each other.

Given no personal background on her he was in the dark, but if he'd had to guess he'd have concluded that she was either normally high-strung or suffering from serious guilt. He hoped it was not the latter.

Isaac and his captain watched her edge away, then

disappear through a gap in the curtains surrounding the exam area. Their eyes met.

"Was she that uptight when you got here, or have you done something to upset her?" Gavin asked.

"Hey, don't look at me." Isaac raised both hands. "If anything, she's acting a little better than she did at first. Her jitters were so noticeable when I walked in, I asked her if she was new on the job."

"And?"

"And, she said she wasn't."

"Curious. You'd think an experienced trauma nurse would have steadier nerves." His brow knit. "I think I'll run a background check on her, just in case."

"She can't have been responsible for the incident tonight. She was working here, right on schedule, when it went down."

"That doesn't mean some of her friends weren't involved." McCord studied Isaac's leg. "You sure you guided Abby to every bench?"

"Yeah. The area was clean when we'd finished our sweep. She didn't alert until after the press conference had started."

"Okay. We'll concentrate on looking for newcomers to the scene when we get a chance to review the videos. Want me to hang around to give you a lift home?"

Isaac shook his head. "You don't have to bother. Culpeper's not that far. I can call my brother or sister to come get me."

"And miss my big chance to grill you all the way to your place? No way. I want to hear every detail."

"Do you have any info on the device yet?" Isaac asked.

"Other than the fact it was an amateur job, not really. We'll be sending the remnants to Quantico for analysis."

"I guess that's better than deciding it was made by an expert."

Isaac's gaze drifted aimlessly as he mulled over his own observations at the blast scene. Movement caught his attention. He froze, nudged the captain and pointed at the feet and ankles visible on the opposite side of the cubicle's curtain.

Gavin McCord moved silently, swiftly, to yank away the cloth barrier. A woman gasped. Covered her mouth with her hands. The nervous nurse had been eavesdropping on their discussion!

Both officers stared at her, not speaking.

"I—I was just waiting to finish that bandage," she said, hurrying to Isaac's side and pulling on a fresh pair of gloves. "I take it you're through talking."

"For now," Isaac said, turning to his boss. "I'll meet you outside when I'm done here, Gavin. Will you take care of Abby for me?"

"Sure. No problem. I'll get your boot, too."

Isaac tried a slight smile to see if it would relax his nurse. "Is it still a madhouse of reporters out there?"

She nodded, yet didn't meet his gaze directly.

"That reminds me of another thing that struck me as odd," Isaac told his captain in parting. He knew McCord was friendly with Jeffries but he just had to ask. "What made Congressman Jeffries decide to call a press conference so late?"

"He says he decided to go public because his pet anti-crime bill was coming up for a vote in the morning."

"He couldn't have waited until tomorrow?"

"Apparently not. He was allegedly proving to his constituency how much that bill is needed to keep DC safe." McCord touched the brim of his cap and picked up the beagle. "Take your time in here. I'll be waiting outside, asking questions and listening to rumors."

Isaac lay back and let Daniella work on his leg, noting her unsteady fingers. As soon as she stripped off her gloves again, he reached for one of her hands.

"You can tell me," he said tenderly.

She pulled away. "Tell you what?"

"Why you're so afraid."

He thought she was going to leave the room without replying until she said, "I just hate bombs, that's all. They're so indiscriminate. So lethal."

"This one wasn't much, if that helps any."

"People were still hurt." After a barely perceptible shiver she continued. "The doctor has released you. You should see your family physician for a follow-up in a few days. Watch for redness, swelling or discharge from the wound and keep it clean and dry."

"Yes, ma'am. Can I walk without crutches?"

"Your leg will hurt more in a few days than it does now but walking won't do any more damage, if that's what you're asking. The injection we gave you will get you home tonight. After that you can take one of the pills in this envelope every four to six hours or switch to over-the-counter painkillers. Just don't double up."

"Anything else?"

"I would say, 'Get a different job,' but I can tell that's not an option for a man like you."

"A man like me? What kind would that be?"

"One who's strong-willed and sure of himself, a person who never wastes time rehashing the past and thinks he's invincible."

"Maybe I really *am*," Isaac teased.

The heartrending look in her emerald-green eyes penetrated his defenses despite his strong resolve. It had been a long time since he'd seen that much poignancy and sorrow in a person's gaze.

This shy, quiet woman had given his heart a twist without saying a word.

Daniella was in no hurry to return to the hospital's common areas, where she could be spotted. Yes, her father's promised vendetta might have vanished with the passage of years but she wasn't willing to take that chance. As her US marshal handlers had warned, leaving the witness protection program was not optional. Once you were in, you stayed. Period.

"Which is the whole point," she murmured. "Having a long and happy life." It was only at times like tonight, when violence brought her past peril to mind, that she fretted so uncontrollably.

Hurrying through the halls, she had almost gained sanctuary when she was paged to go back and assist another doctor. The way she saw her predicament, all she had to do was reach that particular private exam room without passing any nosy reporters or photographers who might inadvertently broadcast her picture and cause untold damage by revealing her hidden identity. Under normal circumstances it would not have been difficult to dodge them. Given the presence of the congressman and his entourage, plus the press corps, moving around in the ER could prove tricky.

Daniella grabbed an extra clipboard, held it beside her cheek to mask her features and hurried toward her new assignment. She was looking ahead so intently she missed noticing a dark-haired figure to her blinded left. She and the muscular man came together with a thump and he grabbed her.

It was all she could do to keep from screaming.

"Hey, settle down," he said. "It's me, Isaac. Are you okay?"

His voice sent tingles racing from the arm he was holding all the way to her toes. Regaining her balance, she helped steady him in return.

"Sorry. I hope I didn't hurt you. I thought you'd already left," Daniella said.

"I was trying to catch up to you and thank you."

"You're quite welcome. Just doing my job."

Before the K-9 cop could reply, she was blinded by an intense flash of light and someone shoved a microphone in her face. "Are you working on the congressman?" a reporter demanded. "Did he really have a heart attack? What's his prognosis? How soon can we see him?"

Isaac's immediate intervention—his arms outstretched and his badge in hand—sent the crowd back a few steps, providing an escape route for Daniella. She held the clipboard between herself and the others and ducked in the exam room door, slamming it behind her.

Her back pressed against the door. She fought to see through the orbs of color that danced in her vision after the camera flashes.

"Over here, Dunne," the doctor said. "I want you to prepare Congressman Jeffries for an X-ray of his shoulder and an EKG, just in case his pain is the result of strain on his heart. I'll send a tech down to take him to radiology. Stay with him until then."

"Yes, Doctor."

"And pull yourself together," he whispered behind his hand in passing. "The last thing our patients need is to hear you shrieking."

"What? When?"

"Just before you opened the door."

"I—I didn't scream. Did I?"

"You made enough noise for me to hear you in here," he said, shooting her a look of disdain. "See that it doesn't happen again. Understood?"

"Yes, sir."

Tall, gray-haired Harland Jeffries was removing his dress shirt and carefully folding the sleeves together before laying the garment aside atop his expensively tailored suit jacket and silk tie.

"You'll need to wear one of our gowns for your tests," Daniella said. "Would you like me to assist you in removing your T-shirt?"

"Fine."

Jeffries's reply was gruff but she wasn't offended. Illness or injury often brought out the worst in patients. *Except for the K-9 cop*, she added. It was really nice of Isaac to step up and physically defend her the way he had. Instead of him thanking *her*, she should be the one dishing out thanks. She owed him. Big-time.

Gently easing the stretchy, white cotton shirt over the congressman's head, she glanced at his back. One side showed a nasty scar from the time he was shot several months ago, sadly at the same time his son, Michael, was murdered.

The opposite shoulder bore an interesting café au lait mark near the scapula. Judging by its odd shape, she guessed it to have been present from conception and birth rather than being another scar or a discoloration caused by trauma.

Daniella fitted the gown around her patient and stepped back. "All right, Congressman, you're ready. I'll wait here with you, as the doctor said, until they come to escort you to radiology."

"Whatever."

His off-putting attitude was nothing like his public

persona. If he had behaved this way toward the press, he'd have killed his chances for reelection long ago.

Thoughts of people who were not trustworthy and genuine reminded her of her childhood. That was all it took to bring back images of the deadly explosion her father had orchestrated.

Yellow billowing fire had leaped and curled back on itself while black smoke roiled. Pieces of metal had rained down. She flinched, wanting to throw her arms over her head and duck just as she had that fateful day her mother had been brutally murdered.

Thankfully, the radiology tech appeared at the door with a wheelchair and distracted both Daniella and her patient.

"Ready, sir?" the tech asked.

"I suppose so." Settling himself in the chair, the congressman pasted a resigned expression on his face, raised his chin and visibly prepared to meet his public. "All right. Let's go."

Daniella waited until the hall was empty before she slipped out. She didn't have to be a licensed physician to suspect that Jeffries was either faking or at least making more of his condition than was warranted. There was no way that man was having heart trouble the way he'd indicated.

Then again, she was very good at spotting falsehoods. After all, she'd grown up in a household where her father's lies were the norm. He was no businessman in the sense he'd implied. His business was crime and his methods for controlling his family were violent. She should know. When he'd tired of abusing her poor mother, he'd graduated to trying to keep Mama in line by hitting Daniella.

That was what had eventually caused her mother to

call it quits and file for divorce. And that was also what had inevitably led to her murder.

To this day, Daniella wondered. If she had been courageous enough to run away when she was younger, would her mother still be alive? Was it all her fault?

Logic said no. Guilt had a different opinion.

Isaac was already beginning to feel the effects of his injury and the pain medication as Gavin drove him out of downtown DC, proving that the decision to let someone chauffeur him home was a wise one. Abby lay on the second seat, content to nap during the short trip.

"It's a good thing your brother and sister live with you," the captain said.

Isaac nodded and stifled a yawn. "Yeah, that's us. The Three Musketeers, 'One for all and all for one.'"

"Must be interesting deciding who's in charge. Do you do it by age or former military rank?"

Chuckling, Isaac shook his head. "We tried both after we inherited the place from our great aunt, but it didn't work very well. We each have our strong and weak points. Jake is a great manager so we leave the running of the farm to him. Becky got into real estate when we were selling off some small lots to help with back taxes and repairs. It suited her so that's what she's doing now."

"And you're the only one in law enforcement."

"Right. Me and Abs." He glanced over his shoulder at his napping partner. "She's a real treasure."

"You need to find somebody like my Cassie."

"Uh-uh. Women are too complicated. Besides, I have Abby and my job."

"That's not enough."

"You underestimate the positive influence of a happy beagle," Isaac replied. "She gives great kisses, too."

McCord rolled his eyes and chuckled. "Sometimes, Black, you really worry me."

Groggy from the pain meds, Isaac yawned again. "Yeah. Sometimes I worry about myself, too."

He closed his eyes, intending to rest, and was surprised to visualize the face of the pretty nurse he'd just met. There was something about her that called out to him; that spoke to his inner man the same way wounded warriors in the VA hospital did. She was haunted, but by what? Or whom?

Isaac blinked and forced himself awake to ask, "Are you still planning on investigating my nurse's background like you said earlier?"

"I think I should, don't you?"

"Yes." There was no way Isaac could make himself doubt Daniella's apparently good character, yet he was curious about what was frightening her. She was plainly scared to death. And judging by the way she'd tried to keep from being photographed, he assumed she was hiding from something. Something that had cut to the core and left her shell-shocked.

Whatever her problem was, or had been, he was determined to learn enough to help her. That kind of thing wasn't in his official job description, at least not for the K-9 unit. It was, however, part of his Christian faith and upbringing. If a neighbor needed assistance, it was his duty to render it to the best of his ability.

Turning his back on the problem was not an option. The good Lord had brought Daniella Dunne into his life for a reason. Now all he had to do was figure out what that reason was and decide whether or not he could do anything for her.

A lot would depend upon what they learned from the

background search. After that, he'd pray about it and make his final decision.

Truth to tell, Isaac thought, smiling as he dozed off, he wasn't going to mind becoming involved in the nurse's troubles. Not one bit.

THREE

The rising sun was painting the sky in streaks of pink and gold before Daniella felt calm again. She had volunteered to stay past the end of her regular shift, just in case there were more bombs or other emergencies, but had ended up idle for most of the rest of the night.

She had considered sleeping at the hospital and not going home at all. If it hadn't been for the needs of Puddy, her black Persian tomcat, she might have opted to stay there indefinitely.

Bone weary, she yearned for solace and privacy and for the quiet companionship of her feline roommate. Her senses were already dulling and she knew that lack of adequate sleep would affect her more and more as the hours passed. She owed her patients her best. The only sensible choice was to give up and go home.

She'd picked up her Windbreaker and purse when someone shouted from the break room. "Hey, everybody! Come here. Look. We're famous."

Daniella joined the rush to peer at the TV screen. A rapid progression of scenes with smoke and a booming sound were followed by pictures of an ambulance, then the inside of the very ER where they all worked.

"There I am." One of the ambulance attendants cheered.

"That should prove to my girlfriend that I really was working last night."

Daniella held her breath. The camera panned. She recognized other staff members. There had been more than one news group present so this airing was no guarantee that she had escaped being photographed. Nevertheless, not seeing herself was a good start. If the other major stations were running pooled footage, all the better.

Just as she started to turn away, someone tapped her arm. "Wow! Look at our Daniella acting like a pop diva."

"What?" Her jaw dropped. Not only had she been caught facing the camera, but the white paper on the clipboard next to her cheek highlighted her features. Even someone who barely knew her would recognize her in that shot.

She sagged against a wall. Moving to a big city was supposed to help her blend in. She liked living in DC. Loved her job and her apartment and the people at work, even the sourpusses. Acceptance of others had accompanied thankfulness for survival and the realization that she was getting a second chance.

Was she going to have to give it all up? Did she dare stay; stand her ground? What were the chances that her father or one of his former cohorts would recognize her on TV and track her down? She'd changed a lot from the gangly teen she'd been back then, but would it be enough?

Wresting the remote from the hand of another nurse, she paused the picture and backed up the scene. There she was, all right. In all her brunette glory. Thank goodness she was still putting a dark rinse on her honey-blond hair.

Daniella ignored murmured protests as she moved the scene forward, then back, then forward again until she was sure of the seriousness of the slipup. In one of the shots her hospital ID badge was visible. It was impossible to read her name as she'd hurried past the reporters, but anyone who had the capabilities to freeze those few frames and enhance the image would also know her false identity.

She clenched her empty stomach and dropped the remote. With one hand clamped over her mouth and the other clutching the strap of her purse, she wheeled and ran from the room.

At his murder trial, ten years ago, her own father had threatened to kill her. Even though he was still in prison, she figured he could hire an assassin. She had done nothing wrong and yet she was serving a longer sentence than he was. She was going to have to keep running and hiding for the rest of her life.

It wasn't fair. She was one of the good guys. This nightmare was *not* supposed to be haunting her.

Isaac didn't remember much about his ride home with Gavin at the wheel and he was asleep minutes after his head hit the pillow. When his phone rang midmorning he was surprised to note how long he had slept.

He answered, "Black."

"How's the leg?" his captain asked.

"Now that you mention it, it hurts. The pain meds I took last night must have worn off."

"Good. You may want to drive and you'll need a clear head."

"I can't drive to work. You carjacked me. Remember?"

"I had your unit delivered to you this morning."

"Are you serious? You really want me to come in today?"

"I have something I think you'll want to see. Of course, I could email the file to you."

"Wanna give me a clue? I'd hate to get dressed and drive all the way into the city for nothing."

"It's about your girlfriend."

"My *what*?" Isaac was sitting on the edge of the bed by now, running his fingers through his hair and taking mental stock of his injury.

"The nurse you wanted me to check on."

"Okay. Go ahead."

"She has a spotless record at the hospital and graduated from nursing school at the top of her class."

"So? That doesn't sound bad."

"Her career is not the most interesting part of her past," McCord said. "Prior to entering college ten years ago, Daniella Dunne didn't exist."

"That's impossible."

"It is if she's on the up-and-up. I don't know who she was before or where she came from. All I know is she's not who she implies she is."

There had been a time when Daniella had tried to keep close tabs on her jailed father. Then, as the years had passed, she had slowly stopped worrying about him and had gone on with her life, content to have a purposeful career and to be a truly new person.

Now, however, she felt it was vital that she know more about the man, if only to set her mind and heart at ease. There was no sense panicking and going on the run if it wasn't necessary. For all she knew, he might have died in prison.

One phone call would tell her everything. The question was, if she did contact the emergency number her original US marshal contact had provided, would she be opening Pandora's box?

She hesitated, her cell phone gripped tightly. Then,

before she could make up her mind whether or not to call for information, the phone rang. Caller ID was no help. All it showed was Unknown.

Could it be the marshal's office taking care in case the call was being monitored? Logically, that might be possible, particularly if she were at work. There was only one way to find out.

She clicked the green button and pressed the phone to her ear. "Hello?"

A low menacing chuckle was followed by, "Well, well. Remember how I always taught you to finish what you started?"

She knew instantly who was on the line. Her father had tracked her down. "How—how did you get this number?"

"I have friends in many places." He laughed again. "I'll see you soon, girl."

Daniella was speechless. That awful voice! Not only did he have her cell number, he probably also knew her address!

Staring at the tiny screen, she noted that he'd ended the call.

Her hands shook and her legs were close to collapse. Every sense insisted that she flee. Immediately. She glanced around at her cozy home. The mere thought of leaving all this behind made her sick to her stomach. Not only would she be in limbo once more, she'd have to give up her friends and career and maybe even her pet, since Puddy was microchipped and might be traceable via his former veterinarian.

She sank into the closest chair and cradled her head in her hands. Although she would have welcomed the release brought by tears, there were none. Numbness and disbelief filled her to overflowing, leaving room for nothing else.

Her first change of identity, when she'd fled Florida as a teen, had been easy compared with what she was facing now. She had often tried to imagine what it would be like to have to abandon nursing and relocate again, but nothing had prepared her for the chilling reality she now acknowledged.

Her murderous father had tracked her down. Life as she'd known it was over. Period.

Isaac was driving himself toward headquarters when his captain radioed Daniella's home address.

"That's right on my way," he replied. "Okay if Abby and I make a stop there, first?"

"Officially?"

"Not exactly. Our mysterious woman may be more willing to fill in some information gaps if I approach her casually."

"It's worth a try. I've already checked with the hospital. She stayed on duty all night so she should be at home now. Just keep us posted. I don't want you going off the grid."

"Who? Me?"

McCord laughed. "Yes, you. Remember that case last fall when you forgot to radio your position and almost got yourself killed before backup could reach you?"

"That was an exception. Getting hurt at the scene last night was not my fault, either," Isaac insisted, noting the dull throbbing in his injured calf. "I followed all the rules precisely. Somebody obviously breached the police security lines after Abby and I checked. If she hadn't acted funny we might have ended up with a lot more casualties."

"You'll get no argument from me on that score," his captain said.

"Good. Listen. I'm almost to the nurse's. I'll have my cell and Abby with me but I'm leaving the rest of my gear in the unit."

"You sure that's wise?"

"Hey, you didn't find any connection between her and terrorists, did you?"

"Not in the last ten years, no."

"Then I'm not taking much of a chance." *Besides, I kind of like her*, he added silently. If there had been anything nefarious about her he figured he would have sensed it—and if he hadn't, Abby would have. Of all the partners he'd ever had, human or otherwise, it was the little beagle he trusted the most. People could be swayed by appearances. Dogs looked beyond the obvious and into a person's true heart.

Slowing as his GPS led him to the address, Isaac pulled into the driveway of an apartment complex. McCord had told him Daniella Dunne lived on the first floor. A mailbox check showed names posted for the other occupants but not for her. That, alone, would have struck him as strange. Coupled with the information he'd gotten from headquarters, it stood out like a red flag.

Her apartment sat at the end of a long interior corridor, next to the rear exit door. Isaac called Abby to heel and limped toward it, mentally preparing an opening line to relax the nurse.

He'd paused at her door when he heard a voice inside. Good. The woman was home. If she failed to respond to his knock he'd have further proof that there was something odd about her.

Isaac raised his fist.

At his side, Abby edged backward.

He was frowning and looking down at his dog when

the door was yanked open and Daniella barreled into him so hard he almost lost his balance.

His arms flew out to steady them both. All he managed to say was "Hey..." when she let out a screech that could have made her the star of a horror movie!

"Whoa," Isaac said, grabbing hold of her upper arms while Abby's leash went flying. "Take it easy. I didn't mean to scare you."

The emerald eyes that were staring into his dark gaze reflected so much raw fear he was taken aback. Her scream had become a whimper and tears were beginning to slide down her flushed cheeks.

As unexpectedly as she'd crashed into him, she flung both arms around his neck and held on as if he were her only lifeline from a sinking ship.

Astounded, he nevertheless embraced her gently. "Easy. I've got you. What's wrong?"

All the answer he got was the sound of her gasping for breath, so he turned to place himself between her and the open apartment door. "Is there somebody else inside?"

Daniella shook her head emphatically, then seemed to come to her senses. "I—I have to get out of here."

"What's the hurry?" he asked, holding her away by cupping her shoulders.

She blinked rapidly and swiveled her head to look up and down the hallway before she said, "Because he's coming."

"Who is?"

"That doesn't matter."

"Whoa. Slow down and start from the beginning. Why are you so scared?"

"He—he threatened to kill me."

"When? Why?"

"A long time ago. I put him in jail."

That was enough information for Isaac to make a sensible decision. He slipped an arm around her shoulders and held her protectively. "Okay. Where do you want to go?"

"Away. Anywhere he can't find me."

"I'll drive."

Daniella twisted out of his grip. "No. I need my own transportation, at least until I can get something untraceable."

"Then Abby and I will follow you," he insisted. "Where are you parked?"

"In the back. The blue car right there." She pointed through the heavy glass of the outside door.

Isaac scooped up the dog's leash. "All right. We'll go first and make sure there's nobody lying in wait. You stay here until I give the okay."

Surveying the parking area until he was satisfied it was deserted, he pulled his smaller holdout gun from the ankle holster he always wore and started toward the parked cars. If Daniella was telling the truth, it was his duty to protect her. If she was making up stories in order to evade law enforcement, his job was to keep track of her. Either way, she was not getting out of his sight.

Isaac cautiously drew closer to Daniella's vehicle.

He felt a tug on Abby's leash.

When he looked back and saw the determined little dog firmly planted in a sitting position and staring straight at the blue sedan, he realized his canine partner had just saved at least two lives: his and the frightened woman's.

Abby was *never* wrong. There was no doubt. Someone had planted an explosive device in the nurse's car.

Waiting at the door, Daniella saw the officer returning rapidly and interpreted his closed, somber expression as either anger or angst. In a smooth motion, he encircled her with one arm and had her back inside her apartment without time for discussion, let alone argument.

"I want you to stay put for right now, understand?"

"No. I told you. I have to leave."

"Not in that car, you don't." He hooked a thumb over his shoulder to indicate her sedan. "I've notified local police. I'm going back outside with my dog to guard the scene until the regular officers relieve me. After that, we can go wherever you want."

"Police? What are they for? I already told you…"

"I don't care what you did or who's after you, lady. Pull yourself together and listen to me. My dog sensed a problem in or around your car, and nobody is going to touch it until the bomb squad has had a chance to look it over. Am I clear?"

She wanted to answer verbally but her body refused to cooperate. There was no breathable air in the apartment. The walls were closing in on her.

She staggered back until she felt her legs contact the front edge of the sofa cushions, then plopped down on them with a whoosh. Her jaw hung slack. Her eyes refused to focus properly. This was even worse than she'd imagined. If Isaac Black had not arrived at just the right moment, she'd have gotten into her car, just as her mother had, and then…

Tears gathered in Daniella's eyes and spilled silently down her cheeks. Her voice was thready. "Are—are you sure?"

"No. But Abby is and that's good enough for me. Now, stay put and let me take care of everything." He drew the living room blinds while his sweet-tempered dog wagged her tail and licked Daniella's fingers.

When he returned and gathered up the leash, he paused with one hand on the doorknob. "Lock this after me."

Her "Okay" was little more than a weak whisper, but at the moment she couldn't manage anything more forceful.

"It'll be all right," Isaac assured her. "Just sit tight and don't move."

"Can I pack a few things?"

"No!" was almost a shout. "Listen carefully. We know that couch is safe because Abby didn't react to it, but I don't want you wandering around in here until I've had a chance to let her explore every room."

"You—you think there's a bomb in here, too?"

"Probably not. But are you willing to take the chance?"

"No. Of course not." She whisked away her tears with the back of her hand.

"Good. Now you're being sensible."

The door closed quietly behind the K-9 officer. Daniella twisted the dead bolt, listening to its click for added assurance. She was safe, at least for the present.

The fortuitous arrival of Isaac and his remarkable dog still amazed her. Could God have somehow spurred him to make this impromptu visit?

She shook her head, clenching her jaw tightly. *No.* God might protect innocent people, but she was far from naive. Her lack of initiative had gotten her mother killed, and her foolish choices afterward had sent her into perpetual hiding.

Although she had no trouble praying for others, she'd long ago given up asking the Lord to watch over or guide her.

Ella Fagan, aka Daniella Dunne, didn't deserve God's love or his forgiveness. The most she could hope for was the wisdom to once more escape her father's vendetta.

Her whirling thoughts would not, could not, carry her further than that.

For all she knew, there would be no life beyond the next few days.

FOUR

With local police waiting outside for the bomb squad, Isaac returned to the apartment. When there was no response to his light knock, he rapped harder.

"Who is it?"

"Isaac Black and Abby."

The moment Daniella opened the door, he smiled. "Good job. I'm glad you're being so careful."

"Careful?" She made a wry face. "I'm scared to even breathe, thanks to you. Do you really think there's another bomb in here?"

"No, I don't. But letting me and Abby check the apartment while you sit on the couch and stay out of trouble is the smartest choice."

She shrugged. "Okay."

His attention now fully on Daniella, Isaac noted that she was wearing jeans and a T-shirt instead of her hospital scrubs. He scowled. "You changed clothes since your shift?"

"Yes, after I got home this morning and showered. Since I was so wide-awake I was planning to run a few errands before taking a nap. I'm almost out of cat food."

"You've already been in the bedroom?"

"Yes." He saw her blanch as reality grew.

"All right. How many cats do you have?"

"Just one. Puddy is black with long hair." She eyed Abby. "Don't let your dog scare him. He doesn't have all his claws."

"I'll keep Abs on a leash." Isaac started for the closest room, the kitchen, noting that it led to a hallway. "This will only take a few minutes. If she doesn't react we'll be right back."

"What if she does?"

"If she does, then we'll both go out the front door and I'll have the bomb squad come in here, too."

"Terrific." Daniella made a silly face.

Isaac had to smile again. "It's good to see that your sarcastic side is still operational."

"It's a coping mechanism a lot of nurses have, I guess."

"So do cops. Civilians don't usually understand how much it helps us when we have to deal with crime and loss so often."

It was clear from the expression on her face that Daniella understood perfectly. Whatever her full background was, she was a sensible and, he hoped, a reasonably stable person. Why that should be important to him was somewhat of a puzzle. Logically, however, she needed a temporary safe house, and he had plenty of extra room on the old farm. Unless Captain McCord came up with some heinous crimes in her past, there should be no reason why he couldn't take her home with him, at least for now. His sister might even have some clothes that would fit her and perhaps change her image enough that she'd be less easily spotted by whoever was menacing her.

His plans were almost fully formed by the time Isaac returned to the living room. "All clear," he said. "I'm satisfied that there's no danger in this apartment right now.

You can go pack but don't take too long. The sooner we get out of here, the better."

"*We?* Where did that come from?"

"I'm taking you home with me—unless you have a better idea."

"I can't go with you. Not just like that."

"Why not?"

"Because you don't really know me."

Isaac smiled wryly. "If I did, should I be afraid of you?"

"Of course not, but…"

"Then it's settled. I'll go put Abby in the SUV, tell the local police what we're doing and be back in a flash. I'll expect you to be ready to leave by then."

"You're *ordering* me to go with you?"

His smile widened. "No. I'm offering a lifeline to a drowning citizen. You can always swim off into shark-infested waters by yourself if you choose."

"I see your point. All right," Daniella said, "but we have to take Puddy. I'm not abandoning him."

"Do you have a carrier?"

"Yes."

"Then put him in it and I'll take him, too."

She began to call, "Puddy? Here kitty, kitty." There was no response. Not even a faint meow.

The stricken look on her face touched Isaac. "I didn't see him when I searched. Maybe he hid when he spotted Abby. I'll take her outside. Keep calling to him while you're packing. Just try not to sound overly anxious. Okay?"

"Okay."

Isaac waited until he heard the door lock click into place before heading down the hall. Getting Daniella to agree to leave her apartment had not been too difficult. Getting her to actually go if she couldn't locate her missing cat might prove far more perplexing. For all they knew, whoever had placed the bomb by the car might have also let the cat out. Anything was possible.

At present, his fondest hope was that the frightened feline would show up.

Daniella was frantic. She faced Isaac, eyes wide, short of breath. "I can't find him. He's not here!"

"Was the door locked when you got home?"

"Of course it was." She frowned. "At least I think so. I was so tired I really didn't pay much attention."

"You weren't scared at that point. So what set you off before I got here?"

Although she hated to answer, she felt she owed him a little more information. "I got a threatening phone call," she said, continuing to search for Puddy while she talked.

Isaac followed her. "Maybe it was a prank."

She shook her head so dramatically her hair brushed against each cheek in turn. "No way. This was for real."

"You know who called?"

"Yes. What I can't figure out is how he managed to get my number so fast. I was only on the news a few hours ago." She explained about seeing herself on TV as part of the coverage about the bombing.

"Maybe he saw you and hacked into the hospital's personnel files."

"I suppose that's possible."

Studying the officer, she could tell he was thinking as various expressions flashed across his face.

"All right," Isaac finally said. "Here's what I know. There is no record of you before you entered college. No high school or grammar school transcripts. Nothing. That means you're either a criminal on the run or a witness who was given a new identity. My guess would be the witness."

Without giving it much conscious thought, she nodded and lowered her gaze, unwilling to meet his directly.

"So why are you acting guilty?"

"Because my family is involved in the whole mess."

"Criminally?"

"Not my mother. She was an innocent victim. My father murdered her."

She heard him draw a quick breath. "And you saw it happen?"

Another nod. She blinked back unshed tears as she raised her face to look at him, hoping to see neither condemnation nor pity. His expression was more quizzical than anything, so she explained further.

"My dad was doing business with some very bad people, drug dealers and hardened criminals. Mom wanted to leave him, we both did, but I was in my teens and I kept hesitating, hoping there was some spark of good left in him."

"That's understandable. He was your father and you were still a kid. You didn't want him to be evil."

"Exactly." She sniffled and continued while peering behind the sofa for the cat. "It was a sunny Sunday afternoon when everything came to a head. Mom told him we were both going to leave for keeps. She started to get into her car. I should have been with her but Dad sent me back into the house to bring him something. I never dreamed he'd already…"

"He saved your life?"

"Yes. But he took hers. The authorities proved he'd rigged an explosive device under her car. I wasn't allowed in court until it was my turn to testify so I don't know whether it was set to go off when she got behind the wheel or if he set it off remotely."

"You testified against him," Isaac said. It was not a question.

Daniella nodded slowly, purposely. "Yes. I had to. A man like that didn't deserve to walk the streets."

"And now you wonder if he might have been released?"

She shrugged. "I can't believe that's possible. Not yet, anyway. I'd rather think he hired someone to terrorize me in his place—except for the fact I recognized his voice on the phone."

"Let's start by finding out for sure where he is. Keep looking for the cat. I'll be right here," he told her, pulling his cell from his pocket and pushing a preprogrammed number. "Give me his full name."

She barely managed to whisper it.

As she worked her way back into the bedroom to search the closet once more, she heard Isaac say, "I need to check on a convict. Terence R. Fagan. If he's been released we need to locate him. Fast."

Daniella paused for a deep, telling sigh. The urge to pray that God would intervene and save her by somehow eliminating her father was strong. And wrong, she knew, yet the disturbing thoughts continued to whirl through her mind. She should be praying for the faith and strength to forgive him, to show him the kind of pure love Jesus demonstrated.

Truth was, she was a long way from that degree of forgiveness and there was no way she'd be able to pray and ask such a thing, not even if her father came to her on his knees and begged.

Surely God understood, she concluded, realizing almost immediately that she was violating one of the important yet simple instructions in the Lord's Prayer.

To be forgiven she must first forgive.

Clenching her jaw and her fists, Daniella refused. There was no way she was ever going to get over what that terrible man had done.

Her broken, battered heart wouldn't allow it.

The news Isaac received in the ensuing few minutes floored him. Terence Fagan had won early release on a technicality and had been roaming the streets for several years. Whether or not he might have located his daughter before her TV news appearance was a moot point. Circumstances seemed to point to a real, present danger. That was all that mattered. The details would eventually sort themselves out.

"Ms. Dunne," Isaac called as soon as he'd ended his phone conversation. "Come on. We have to go. There's no time to waste."

She poked her head around the corner into the kitchen. "I can't go yet. I'm not leaving without Puddy."

"Yes, you are."

The mist filling her eyes made them glisten like jewels in the rain. "No. Please. I know he's here. He has to be."

"Unless someone let him out while they were trying to break in." Isaac saw little chance of that but persisted. "Why don't you leave dishes of food and water in the usual place in here, then put others in the hallway, just in case? I'll either stop by to check or have members of my team do it. Puddy will show up as soon as he gets hungry enough. The problem is, you can't stay here and wait for that to happen."

She stared at him, her hands trembling.

He approached her slowly, hoping to keep her as calm

as possible when he delivered the bad news. Stopping an arm's length from her, he looked deeply into her eyes, willing her to continue to trust him, at least enough to heed his sage advice.

Her eyes widened. "What are you not telling me?"

"That call I just made? It was to our tech support. Terence Fagan has been out of prison for several years."

"That's impossible!"

Isaac lightly cupped her elbow to steady her. "I'm sorry. It's true. His appeal was granted on a technicality."

She swayed as if dizzy, so he continued to hold her arm, just in case. "No. Your information must be wrong."

"Sorry. Our Fiona Fargo is the best computer tech in the business. If she says your father has been released, he has been."

"Why wasn't I told?"

"I don't know. When you get in touch with the marshals' office to arrange to be moved, you can ask them. It was probably an oversight."

"Oversight? This is my *life* we're talking about."

Isaac nodded soberly. "I'm glad you realize that." He let go and opened her cupboards to locate usable dishes. "Will these do for your cat?"

She barely nodded.

"Okay. I'll fill one with water and you put dry food in the other so we can be on our way."

This time she not only didn't argue, she moved to comply as if in a stupor. That state of mind wasn't any better for her than her earlier panic, although it did make his current task easier.

Until they could coordinate with the US Marshals office in DC, his best option would be to take her home with him, as he'd already been planning.

There was more than one good reason for that choice,

too. His injured leg was starting to really throb and the sooner he was free to take his prescribed medication the better he'd feel.

Reasoning that a nurse would be sympathetic and therefore more compliant, he decided to tell her. "Listen, I hate to mention this but I'm starting to feel awfully sore. I couldn't chance taking my morning meds and getting behind the wheel of a motor vehicle so I haven't had any painkillers since what you gave me last night."

That snapped her out of her doldrums enough to frown and caution, "You should have kept up with them. It's not just for comfort, you know. Controlling pain will help you heal faster. Plus, one of those scripts was for oral antibiotics."

"Afraid I didn't stop to look," Isaac admitted. "When my captain called me, I didn't question his reasons."

"What was he *thinking*? You're injured."

Isaac chanced a slight smile. "Actually, it was my decision. He told me he was worried because there was no record of your past and wanted to confer with me."

"That's a lame excuse if I've ever heard one," Daniella said. Hoisting a bulging tote bag, she sighed as she started for the door. "I won't be responsible if you develop an infection. Let's go."

Following her out the apartment door and waiting while she carefully relocked it, Isaac couldn't help feeling relieved and more than a little glad. She was finally thinking more clearly. That was a definite plus.

Now all he had to do was take a small enough dose of painkiller to allow his own brain to function properly and they'd be a formidable team.

Visualizing himself and Daniella as a team caught him by surprise. They had little if anything in common, so why was he seeing her as part of his work, let alone his life?

Because the effects of this injury have addled me, he concluded. That aberration would surely pass.

His smile waned. *It had better.* In his line of work, letting a pretty face distract him could be fatal.

Since there was a logo on the door of the SUV that matched the patches on Isaac's uniform shirt, it was easy for Daniella to tell which official vehicle belonged to the K-9 cop. None of the responding agencies had pulled into the apartment driveway. Consequently, the street was blocked both ways.

She looked to him as they walked. "How did you know to park so far away?"

"I didn't. I moved my car for safety when I put Abby inside."

"Oh. I thought for a second…"

"That I was part of the plotting against you?"

"I never considered it seriously," she alibied. "I'm just jumpy."

"That's perfectly understandable."

"What else can you tell me about my father? You're absolutely positive he's out of prison?"

"Yes. His attorney filed an appeal and got his sentence reduced because of some glitch in the gathering of evidence at the crime scene. He pleaded guilty to providing the plans for the explosive device but insisted some of his cronies had actually made, planted and detonated it because they wanted to get rid of *him*, not your mother."

"Then why did he send me into the house at just the right moment to save my life?"

"He claimed it was a coincidence."

That statement gave her pause. Finally, she said, "If that's true, you know what it means, don't you?"

Isaac nodded as he opened and held the passenger door for her. "Yes. If he was being honest about his innocence, he wasn't showing his love, like you thought, by keeping you away from your mother's car."

As she slipped into the seat, she wished there weren't unshed tears threatening to trickle down her cheeks.

Daniella waited until Isaac was behind the wheel before she commented further. "Dad set that bomb. I know he did. The expression on his face wasn't surprise or shock after it went off, it was victory."

She sniffled and swiped at her damp cheeks. "He killed Mom as surely as I'm sitting here." Sighing, she stared out the SUV's window.

"That doesn't really explain why he'd be causing you trouble after all this time," Isaac offered.

"Sure it does. That man never forgave a soul. After I testified against him he swore he'd get even. That's why I agreed to go into witness protection in the first place."

"You believe he meant what he said?"

Daniella huffed and set her jaw. "Oh yeah. Of all the things he ever told me, that's the one promise I know he intends to keep."

"I'm sorry," Isaac said.

She knew she'd start to sob if she saw pity in the officer's eyes, so she kept staring out the window.

The voice on the phone had been unmistakable. Her father was on her trail and closing in. Every moment that passed was one more she had managed to eke out.

And brought her one more breath closer to her last if Terence Fagan had his way.

FIVE

Once they were past the beltway, the country quickly turned to farmland. Isaac waited to give the pastoral scenes a chance to calm his companion. When he finally spoke, it seemed to startle her.

"How're you doing?"

"Oh!" Her head whipped around. "Sorry. I guess I was daydreaming."

"That's better than some of the things you could have been thinking about. We're almost home."

"It's pretty out here. I just have trouble picturing you as a farmer."

He chuckled. "I'm not. My sister, brother and I inherited the place from an aunt and decided to fix it up to sell. That was five years ago and we're still there."

"*We?* You don't live alone?"

Isaac could see her relief. He laughed. "Nope. I'm not inviting you home for disreputable reasons. My sister, Becky, will see to it that Jake and I behave. I can guarantee it."

"Are they older or younger than you?"

"Jake's older. Becky's younger, but not by much. Our parents had us close together so we'd get along better, and it apparently worked because they're my best friends."

"Except for Abby, you mean."

"Right. Abs and I are best buds."

"How long have you worked with her?"

"A little over two years, counting the training. I was recruited for the K-9 unit by General Margaret Meyer after I left my other government job."

"Which was?"

Her expression was so open and innocent looking he answered without hesitation. "I worked for the CIA."

"You were a *spook*?"

Letting his amusement show, he shook his head. "Actually, I spent most of my time training dogs to be sent into the field, until someone decided I belonged in an office, organizing the whole project."

"No wonder you wanted to get a different job. I couldn't stand being stuck behind a desk, either." She took a deep breath and released it with a whoosh. "What am I going to do? I love being a trauma nurse and working ER."

"So, you tell that to the marshals and insist they find you another similar position."

"What if they won't? Suppose they feel it's too dangerous? I mean, wouldn't that make it easier to trace me?"

"Maybe, maybe not. Don't borrow trouble, Daniella. There's enough of it already around."

"That sounds biblical."

"Probably. My folks were pretty religious."

"Were? Are they gone?"

"Sadly, yes. They were both killed in a traffic accident while all of us were stationed away. Jake was a marine and Becky flew for the air force."

"Really? That's impressive. I'm sure you all made your parents proud." Her smile faded and Isaac could see the light going out of her eyes. "My mother was always proud of me but I could never please my father."

"That doesn't mean you weren't worthy," Isaac told her. "It just means that he wasn't a normal dad. You can't blame yourself for his shortcomings."

"I don't, but..."

"No *buts* about it. I've only known you for a little while and I can see you're an extraordinary person. You've overcome adversity to finish college and go on to a rewarding career. You're well liked at work and best of all, Abby thinks you're wonderful. I saw her licking your hands back at your place."

"She's a sweetheart. I was trying to pet her and she seemed to take to me right away."

That makes two of us, Isaac thought. There was something about Daniella that had spoken to his heart the moment he'd met her.

Whether or not that was for the best remained to be seen.

The old farmhouse was far more charming than Daniella had expected. Basically a simplified Victorian, it sported a fresh coat of white paint with red shutters and trim, plus window boxes of early flowers like tulips and pansies.

She grinned. "It's lovely. No wonder you all decided to stay here."

"Believe me, it didn't look half this good when we inherited it," Isaac replied. "Jake has done wonders with the place."

"He must be very talented."

Isaac laughed. "So he claims."

"Sibling rivalry? I have no experience with brothers or sisters. I'd think you'd be proud of him, though."

"I am. We just like to needle each other. You'll see."
He gave a soft chuckle. "Our sister, Becky, is the worst."

"You're sure they won't mind my stopping here for
a few days, at least until I have new instructions from
the marshals? I mean, I wouldn't want to make trouble."

"Believe me, there's no way you'll make more trouble
than the three of us can stir up. We love to tease each
other and pull practical jokes."

A tall, stalwart man in a T-shirt and jeans appeared at
the side of the house, waved and started their way. Daniella could see the family resemblance even though the
second man needed a shave. In spite of this one's rug-
ged image, she judged Isaac to be slightly better-looking.

Jake trotted out to the SUV with a hammer in his
hand, peered in at Isaac's passenger and broke into a
face-splitting grin. "Whoa! Good one, bro. You head
for the office to work even though you're stove-in and
bring home a pretty lady. That's what I call a good job."

Stove-in was right. Moving stiff-legged on his injured
side, Isaac climbed from behind the wheel. Daniella had
opened her own door at the same time so he introduced
her to his brother with a wave. "This is Jake, as you've
probably guessed. Jake, Daniella Dunne. Becky's a lot
prettier than he is. And more polite."

Jake wiped his hand on his jeans before shaking hands
with her, then looked over at his brother. "Girlfriend or
damsel in distress?"

"Damsel, definitely," Daniella answered for him. "The
distress part is true, too."

"Sorry to hear that." Jake's grin faded. "How can we
help you?"

"I'll take care of Ms. Dunne," Isaac interjected. "I'm
going to put her things in Becky's room for now. Later,

the women can work out whatever arrangements suit them."

"Ooooh-kay. You play cop while I finish nailing up the new cabinets in the washroom." Jake started away, then stopped and turned. "Don't run off and forget Abby. I'd hate to see you get so involved with a pretty face that your dog suffers."

"I'd never do that," Isaac insisted. Clenching his jaw, he let the little beagle out of the traveling crate he sometimes used and removed her working harness before releasing her and picking up his houseguest's tote.

Abby's sharp yaps brought larger dogs running. Daniella ducked behind Isaac, her hands resting lightly on his shoulders.

"Don't let the dogs scare you," he told her. "They're as gentle as Abs. They just look ferocious."

When she said, "They sound like it, too," her host laughed.

"Stand still and let them sniff you. After that you'll be considered one of the family."

A wiggling brown nose the size of the diaphragm on the business end of a stethoscope touched the knee of her jeans. "I think he smells Puddy."

"That's no problem. We have plenty of cats in the barn and the dogs treat them all with respect, even the kittens."

"You're sure? This one has teeth as big as a wolf."

"The better to protect you with, my dear, to paraphrase the old fairy tale. Make friends with these dogs and any one of them will defend you to the death."

"Interesting choice of words." She rolled her eyes. "What breeds are they?"

"Those two brown-and-black ones are large mutt crossed with very large mutt," Isaac said with a smile. "The third is probably shepherd and yellow Lab. We stick to purebreds for K-9 work because their talents are more predictable, but in private life I like to rescue needy animals."

"Well, I feel like a juicy bone about to be served for supper," she joked, beginning to relax as her furry new acquaintances lost interest in her and dashed off in pursuit of Abby.

Glancing at the open yard, Daniella wished there were more trees and bushes to hide behind. Then again, the lack of a lot of vegetation near the house also meant no one could jump out to pounce on her. On them.

She eyed the long driveway. "You're sure nobody followed us?"

"I'm sure. When I called in to tell my boss what I was doing, I asked for a few of my buddies to run interference, just in case. None of them spotted trouble or they'd have radioed me."

"That's a relief," she said. And it was. Except it was also temporary. Everything in her life was. She was out of a job due to having been identified, she had no home because the apartment was known to her worst enemy, and all her efforts at staying in the shadows had been for nothing. She didn't even have Puddy anymore, and he was the closest thing she had to a real, true friend. One thing was certain. She could not just abandon the cat any more than this K-9 officer would ever give up Abby.

Following Isaac up the wooden front steps to the covered porch, Daniella stopped him with a touch. "Tomorrow, I'm going back to rescue my cat," she said flatly.

"You couldn't find him today. What makes you think you'll succeed tomorrow?"

"Because I'll be going into my apartment alone."

"Over my dead body," Isaac countered.

"Hopefully, it won't come to that," she shot back cynically, calmer now that she'd made a decision to act. Anything was better than feeling helpless and vulnerable.

"Not funny."

"It wasn't meant to be. The more I think about it, the more I realize Puddy was scared of you as well as the dog. If you stay outside and I go in by myself, he should come out of hiding."

"That's assuming he's still in the apartment."

"Yes. It is. I don't buy your idea that somebody let him out. He's always been an indoor kitty. Chances are he wouldn't have run out even if the door was left open."

"Do you have a death wish?" Isaac asked, frowning.

Daniella shook her head. "Tell me. What would you do if Abby was lost in your house and you were about to move away? Would you leave her with food and water and turn your back on her?"

"That's different."

"No, it isn't." She blinked to clear her vision and try to regain more control of her turbulent emotions. "That cat has been my sole companion for over five years. I am not abandoning him. Period. Understand?"

When she saw that she had convinced Isaac, she brushed past him and entered the house. If she failed to honor her commitment to a helpless animal, how could she ever hope to be trusted with the kind of love and acceptance for which she yearned? It was the little things in life that formed a person's character. Sure, traumatic events played a role, but it was small kindnesses and daily thanksgiving that truly shaped people's lives.

And evil acts that tore them apart, she thought sadly. There was nothing she could do to erase the damage her father had done, nor could she forget his wickedness.

But that didn't mean she was going to surrender— to him or to her fear. She wasn't in this alone anymore.

Whether he knew it yet or not, Isaac Black was clearly on her side.

Picturing him boldly stepping between her and the news people, despite his injured leg, she let her imagination equip him with armor and weapons and a trusty steed—tricolored, with floppy ears and a wagging tail!

A combination of nerves and a sense of the absurd brought giggles, then snickers and finally tears that rolled down Daniella's cheeks as she doubled up laughing.

"Would you mind telling me why you find my house so funny?" Isaac asked, sounding a tad miffed.

She could not, would not, tell him, of course. What she did manage to say was, "It's not you or your house. It's me. I think I may be wound a little tight."

He nodded. "Come on. I'll show you to your room and you can rest. I may not be technically at work but I have plenty to do on my laptop." He pointed as they passed a ground-floor room. "If you need me, I'll probably be in there."

"If you give me your cell number I can just phone you," she said, feeling quite clever for having thought of it.

He dropped her tote at the foot of the stairs. "You brought your cell phone?"

"Of course."

"Give it to me."

"No. I may need it."

"So your father can call you again or so he can trace your whereabouts through it?"

"What? That's just TV nonsense, isn't it?" Nevertheless, she placed her phone in his outstretched hand and watched as he removed the battery and the tiny information-processing card.

"I'll turn this over to my people and see if they can

trace your last incoming call. That would be your father, right?"

Mute and subdued, she nodded. In the space of a few moments she had gone from strong and resolute to scared witless again. Her emotions weren't merely on a roller coaster, they were taking a ride on a spaceship that had run out of rocket fuel halfway to the moon and was now plummeting to earth, where it would smash to smithereens.

Daniella gritted her teeth. The imaginary rocket hadn't crashed yet. The ending wasn't written in stone because she wasn't done fighting. Not by a long shot.

Straightening and thrusting back her shoulders, she stood firm and faced Isaac. "I'm sorry. I didn't know."

Surprisingly, his stern features softened as he admitted, "No, but I did. The error is mine. I should have confiscated your phone back at the apartment and turned it over to the authorities."

"Why didn't you?"

"I'd like to blame my injury or the meds I'd been on for the pain but that won't fly—with my boss or with me." He made a face. "As much as I hate to even think it, I suspect I was concentrating too much on you."

"Me?"

She noted the rosy color infusing his cheeks and guessed what he might mean before he said, "Yes, Daniella. You. Only not as a victim or a suspect, as an appealing young woman who interested me. That was my mistake. I promise it won't happen again."

All she could think to say was *too bad*.

Thankfully, good sense kept her from voicing it.

As far as Isaac was concerned, he was still on the job even if his dog wasn't. He offered his guest a quick tour of the ground floor of the old farmhouse, then suggested she get some sleep upstairs in his sister's room while she had the chance.

What he didn't say was that Daniella might need all her strength and wits in the coming hours and days and should take advantage of any opportunity to recover from the long, trying night before.

Limping to the small room he used as a home office, Isaac was more than ready to get off his feet. He propped his sore leg on a half-open drawer, leaned back in the swivel chair and powered up the laptop he normally carried in his work vehicle. A simple password and he was in.

Most of his emails were inconsequential compared with the files McCord had sent about Daniella. A quick scan told him that the captain hadn't left out anything. The gaps were evident, and now that he knew she'd been relocated by witness protection he wasn't surprised.

Getting the old records of her journey from past to present might be hard to do but learning about her father's crimes and punishment was not going to be tough. Fagan's arrest and conviction were matters of public record. He'd start there, then see how much more help he needed to complete his own file on Daniella.

He'd hardly begun when Captain McCord telephoned. "Black. How are you feeling?"

"Sore. And halfway mad at myself. But the nurse is safe now. She's with me."

"Yeah, so I understand. I thought I warned you to not get personally involved."

"She's not staying here long. I just needed someplace to put her while we get in touch with witness protection and they make new plans for her."

"And when will that be?"

"Very soon. The poor woman's at the end of her rope and there's nothing wrong with letting her unwind here. Once she calls the Feds we'll lose jurisdiction."

"You mean you'll lose touch with her, don't you?"

Isaac took a deep breath before he answered, "That has crossed my mind, yes."

"Well, I'll cut you some slack because of your leg. But while you're home playing babysitter you also need to keep on top of our other cases. General Meyer says the White House wants results on the Michael Jeffries murder, for one. With the congressman back in the news because of the bombing at his press conference, reporters have started asking questions about his late son again."

Despite working diligently on the murder case—and the attempted murder of the congressman himself—the Capitol K-9 Unit was no closer to solving it. "I copy. Has there been any more news about the child who may have witnessed the attack at the Jeffries estate?"

Isaac thought about the child's glove that had been found near the crime scene and the subsequent attacks on All Our Kids foster home, which had resulted in the home being moved to a secret location. The Capitol K-9 Unit surmised that the killer had seen a child watching from the tree line of the woods between the congressman's property and the former foster home, but that the killer didn't know *which* child—hence the attacks on the foster home.

"Some. Tommy Benson admitted he snuck out that night and his caretakers report he's been having nightmares."

"Are the children safe at the new location?"

"Yes. Nicholas interviewed Tommy after the boy got spooked by something and ran away from the home. We're positive he's the kid who witnessed Michael Jeffries's murder and dropped the blue glove in the woods. He did say he's afraid of some guy with white hair. That's about all we've managed to get out of him."

Isaac mentally shook his head at the thought of anyone harming the innocent children at the foster home. He pictured little Juan Gomez, the two-year-old son of Congressman Jeffries's former housekeeper, who'd been found dead at the bottom of a cliff the night before Michael Jeffries's murder. Juan had been staying at All Our Kids until a couple of months ago, when his aunt, Lana Gomez, took him in. "What's going on with Juan Gomez? Is he happy living with his aunt Lana?"

"All reports are very positive," the captain said.

"Good. Send me updates and I'll reread the files to refresh my memory, then get back to you if I see anything that gives me new ideas. I still think there may be a connection between Rosa's death and that of the congressman's son."

"Michael Jeffries was an attorney," McCord said flatly. "They make enemies."

"Yeah, but they don't all end up shot and killed."

McCord was adamant. "There's no way the Jeffries family is guilty of anything except being involved in Washington politics. I've known Harland since I was a kid. If I thought for a minute that they'd actually broken the law, I'd be the first to act."

Which is probably a big part of the reason this case is stalled, Isaac thought. He decided it would be best to change the subject. "Okay. I'll call in as soon as we know where Daniella Dunne is going and when."

"Fair enough. Talk to you later."

The conversation over, Isaac sat and pondered the facts he already knew, sharing them with Abby, who never offered unasked-for opinions.

He smiled down at her. "One, Harland Jeffries is as crooked as a dog's hind leg no matter what Gavin thinks. My apologies, girl." The little beagle wagged her tail and made herself comfortable sprawled on the hardwood floor beside him. Research into the congressman's activities hinted at corruption, the taking of bribes, but nothing that could be proven—yet.

"Two," Isaac went on, "Jeffries's longtime housekeeper took a swan dive off a cliff but left no suicide note."

"Three, whoever shot the son evidently also tried to kill the father. Jeffries could have bled out before help arrived."

As he mused, Isaac was absently tickling Abby's soft, floppy ears with the fingers of one hand.

"Four, Erin Eagleton, another daughter of Senator Eagleton, is believed to have been on the scene during the lethal assault because her jewelry was found there." He took a deep breath and released it as a sigh. "And five, there's a scared kid named Tommy who just may have the answers to everything."

Isaac felt as if someone had put his thoughts in a blender and flipped the switch. Even if they did not yet have all the facts concerning these complicated cases, there was a good chance they had enough clues to at least make some headway.

"Somehow, it all has to hinge on Jeffries. He's the only common denominator."

When a feminine voice behind him asked, "What makes you say that?" Isaac jumped and almost fell off his chair.

SIX

Daniella covered a giggle with her hand. "Oops. Sorry. I didn't mean to startle you."

"I thought you were taking a nap."

She shrugged. "That's hard to do when all I can think about is being blown to bits."

Isaac frowned. "You don't feel safe here?"

"Here? Of course," she answered. "But I can't stay forever. I need to call the US marshals and tell them what's happened so they can relocate me."

"I know. Want to borrow my phone?"

"That won't help much. All the specific info I need to identify myself is either on the phone card you got rid of or in my apartment. They don't just arbitrarily believe anybody who calls and claims to be one of their protected witnesses."

"That makes sense. So, what you're saying is that you need to go back there soon." He began to smile wryly, making her feel as if he believed she'd tried to trick him and failed.

"It's *true*."

"I don't doubt it. I'm also sure you've been racking your brain to come up with a plausible reason to go looking for your cat." The smile grew. "Am I right?"

"You've never heard of killing two birds with one stone?"

"Sure. I've also heard of pet owners who consider their animals to be family."

"Ha! You should talk." She made sure he saw her staring at Abby. The beagle had rolled onto her back and was lying with all four legs in the air, begging for a tummy rub.

"I told you before. This dog and I are working partners."

"Well, Puddy's my only true friend so he counts, too." She could tell by the way the officer sobered and straightened in his chair that she'd revealed too much.

"I know you have more good friends than one cat."

Daniella shook her head slowly, deliberately. "No. I don't. I didn't dare let myself get too close to anybody in case this very thing happened. My father is too vindictive. If he thought anyone was important to me, the way Mom was, it would be just like him to eliminate that person out of sheer meanness."

She heard Isaac give a sigh as he turned back to his computer and said, "All right. Let's see what else we can find in your father's background that might help us anticipate his next move. How about known associates? Can you think of people he might contact in civilian life? What about the men he worked with before he was sent to prison?"

"Most of them either died or landed in jail, too. Besides, I told all that to the police and the prosecutor before his trial."

"I don't necessarily mean the criminal element. I mean regular folks. You know, his garage mechanic or the pool boy or yard man. People like that."

She raked her fingers through her hair. "I can't remember. It was ten years ago and I was a self-centered teenager. I hardly noticed those kinds of employees."

"You mean you didn't have a crush on the pool boy?"

Her cheeks warmed. "All I can recall is his dark, wavy hair and nice muscles. Not nearly as nice as yours, though." The warmth of her face increased until she had no doubt she was visibly blushing.

The computer made a chirping noise and drew their attention. Isaac clicked on his email icon and opened the attachment. It contained autopsy photos along with a series of recent reports. "Sorry," Isaac said.

"Hey, I'm a nurse, remember?" She leaned over his shoulder to peer at the screen. "Who is that?"

"Michael Jeffries, Harland's son. Mind if I look at the rest of the file?"

"Not at all. If I hadn't chosen nursing I might have gone into the study of forensics."

As the shots flashed by, she suddenly squeezed Isaac's shoulder. "Stop. Go back. I want to look at that one."

"Looks like Michael hurt his shoulder when he fell."

Daniella pointed. "No, no. That's not an injury. It's a birthmark. I saw one almost identical to it on Harland Jeffries's shoulder just the other night."

"Interesting. Is that kind of thing rare?"

"Not really. Unlike some other types of marks, ones like that can be inherited. It's called a café au lait mark, coffee with cream," Daniella explained. "If I had a picture of Harland's back I could prove it."

"You don't have to prove anything to me. I believe you."

She smiled and gave Abby's stomach a rub.

"About everything," he added. "And I'm going to do my best to see that no harm comes to you."

"Thanks." She didn't pull away when Isaac laid his warm hand over hers and held very still.

He didn't speak again. Neither did she.

There was no need.

Isaac figured he could stall his houseguest and keep her from returning to her apartment for one more day, maybe two. The cat had plenty of food and water so it wouldn't suffer. He simply preferred to keep Daniella away long enough for whoever was after her to determine she was no longer living there.

He sent her out to talk to his brother so he could telephone his sister, Becky, in private. The real estate office answering machine picked up his call.

Instead of listening to the message, he hung up and dialed her cell. "Becky, pick up," he was saying as her "Hello" cut in.

Isaac huffed. "Where are you?"

"On my way to show a house in Arlington. Why?"

"I hope you don't mind having a surprise houseguest."

"Mind? Of course not. Who is it?"

"Daniella Dunne. She's an innocent victim of a crime. She won't be with us long."

"She can stay as long as she needs to. Give her my room if you want. Is there anything else I can do to help her?"

"Come home ASAP," Isaac said. "Daniella acts fine most of the time but I'm getting the idea she's a lot more fragile than she lets on. I don't want her to fall apart with only me and Jake here to comfort her."

Listening to his sister chuckle upset Isaac. "Look, Becky, this is not funny."

"Hey, I was laughing at you, not her."

"Well, fine. Daniella's scared, as she should be, and

until the cops can find the person who set explosives under her car, she'll continue to be in danger."

"How can you be sure of that?"

"Because there's more to the story. The bomb construction was familiar, for one. Crude but effective."

"What about the one that went off last night by the monument? Which reminds me, how's your leg?"

"It hurts. Thanks for asking," Isaac said, tongue in cheek. This was not the first time it had occurred to him to wonder why the two recently set bombs were so similar, both in size and destructive efficiency—or in this case, inefficiency.

"We sent the fragments of the first one to the lab at Quantico," Isaac continued. "I don't know what the bomb squad did with the unexploded one under Daniella's car but I'm sure somebody thought to compare the test results. If not, I'll see it gets done."

"Hmm. This is the second or third time you've called her by her first name. Just how close a friend is she?"

"I met her last night," he said flatly.

"And? That doesn't mean a thing if you've fallen for her already."

"Don't be ridiculous. Nobody can get seriously involved that fast. Not even me."

"Okay, okay. I just thought I heard something different in your voice when you talked about her, that's all."

"No way. You're imagining things." But was she? Isaac wondered. There had been something odd, some unexplainable connection, that he'd sensed the moment Daniella's frightened gaze had locked with his in the ER. They did have an emotional bond of sorts, the kind that appeared once in a lifetime, if ever. He knew it and he suspected that Daniella knew it, too.

Beginning to mutter the moment the call ended, Isaac

pushed himself to his feet and made sure he was steady on his sore leg, then limped toward the area of the house where Jacob was currently at work.

As he approached, he overheard his brother's robust laugh, then the higher, lovelier pitch of a woman enjoying the same uplifting emotion. It had to be Daniella, yet the change in her mood seemed so unlikely, he paused to listen.

"So, grab a hammer and give me a hand," Jake said. "I dare you."

Isaac couldn't make out her answer but he didn't care. There was no way he was going to permit her to hang out with his brother when she should be with him and Abby, where she'd be safest.

Careful to smile as he rounded the corner into the laundry room, Isaac stopped. "There you are. I was getting worried."

Her head slanted in a quizzical pose. "Why? You're the one who sent me to Jake," Daniella countered.

"I know. I just needed privacy. You can come back to the den now."

It floored him when she shook her head and said, "I'd rather stay here and help your brother if it's all the same to you. He needs me to hold the level while he nails things in place."

The urge to make a fuss and insist she rejoin him was so strong Isaac almost expressed his disappointment. He saw Daniella look from him to his brother, then back again, as if she were a child trying to decide which flavor of cookie to choose.

He wanted her to come with him voluntarily rather than because he'd ordered it. What little he already knew about her was contradictory, yet instinct told him she could be stronger than she appeared sometimes. She'd have had to be to survive and thrive after her turbulent teen years. Any weakness he was sensing now had to be mostly due to the reappearance of her lethal father.

Having enjoyed a home with stable, loving parents and a peaceful childhood, Isaac couldn't imagine the pain she must have suffered. Must still be suffering.

Perhaps it was his empathy, perhaps his deep desire to look after her, that made the difference. He didn't care how it was defined. All he knew was that Daniella abruptly turned to Jacob to apologize for leaving, then joined him.

He smiled. She took his arm. The warmth of her touch through the fabric of his shirtsleeve was unbelievable. For a few moments he actually forgot the pain in his leg, overlooking everything but her.

When she said, "You know, it's high time I contacted the marshal's office and set up an appointment," Isaac's heart lodged in his throat.

Of course she was leaving DC. He'd known that from the beginning. So why were his emotions taking him for such an impossible ride?

It must be the pain meds that were befuddling his brain, he concluded. No way was he going to actually fall for a woman whose primary goal was to disappear for good. He was smarter than that.

At least he hoped he was.

Parts of the day sped by for Daniella while other parts seemed interminable. Her biggest concern was for her poor, abandoned kitty.

"I've decided what to do," she began at the dinner table. Becky had arrived bearing several pizzas and the rest of them had set the table. "Do?" Isaac raised a brow.

"About Puddy. You can drop me at my apartment in the morning and I'll go in alone so he won't be so scared."

She saw his gaze rake over his brother and sister before returning to her. "See? What did I tell you? The woman is self-destructive."

"I'm nothing of the kind. I'm logical. Puddy's afraid of dogs. That's why he hid. All I have to do is go in by myself and he'll come right to me. Then I can dig out my private contact numbers for witness protection and I'll be all set."

"Not happening," Isaac muttered.

"Why not?" If she'd been standing she'd have planted her fists on her hips. As it was she almost pounded the dining room table. "You told me there was a watch on my apartment in case my— In case the bad guys showed up again, so unless your cop buddies are slacking off, the place should be secure."

Jake chuckled. "She's got you there, bro."

Agreeing, Becky reached over and patted Daniella's hand. "When you're right, you're right. Would you like me, or all of us, to go with you?"

"Not necessary. But thanks for the offer. Like I said, the cat is kind of shy. Being black, it's easy for him to hide in dark spaces and I'm afraid if I don't coax him out soon he may get depressed and make himself sick."

Laughing softly, Becky winked at her brothers. "Well, guys, I tried to get us invited. Guess you're on your own."

As far as Isaac was concerned this was no laughing matter. He scowled at his siblings. "Coercion isn't necessary. Ms. Dunne wants to survive long enough for the authorities to arrange a new life for her. I'm sure she knows I'm right about not going off on her own." He smiled as if positive she was about to agree. When she did not, he was happy to see the subject dropped, at least temporarily.

He just wished he couldn't see the wheels grinding in her fertile imagination. One look in her eyes told him she was far from convinced.

"Suppose we play it by ear and see what the circumstances are once we get to my apartment," Daniella suggested, eyeing his injured leg after breakfast the following morning. "After all, I know better than to bandage a cut without cleaning it and assessing the damage first. The same should go for your job. It's silly to borrow trouble and react defensively to a threat that may never come about."

Isaac's palms were pressed to the table as if he intended to leap to his feet. Instead, he stood slowly, deliberately. His shoulders were square, his spine stiff and his jaw set, presenting an image of an immovable granite boulder rising from bedrock.

"Ms. Dunne," he began, "I have never lost a person I was assigned to protect and I don't intend to start now. Either you agree to do things my way or we won't do them at all. Am I making myself clear?"

"Perfectly."

Daniella knew she shouldn't fight his good intentions, yet a perverse side of her personality kept insisting she didn't need looking after. Logically, she did, of course. Anyone in his or her right mind could see that. It was just that when Isaac issued orders he got under her skin. Perhaps it was his tone, although it could also be the way he delivered his demands. His body language brooked no argument, actually spurring her to disagree just on principle.

Which is totally unfair, she chided herself, realizing she was being unreasonable—and not liking the picture of herself as a petulant, spoiled child.

Finally she said, "All right, Officer Black. You win. We'll do it your way. Just take me back to find my cat. Please?"

"Of course. As long as you promise to behave reasonably from now on."

Daniella raised her right hand as if taking a solemn oath. "I hereby promise to be reasonable about the rescue of my pet, Puddy." She grinned slyly with a telltale twitch of mirth at the corners of her mouth.

Any vow she took was meant to be kept and there was no way she'd ever agree to promise to do things the officer's way forever. Just getting through the following few days was going to be hard enough without placing further restrictions on her thoughts and actions.

She was her own woman. She'd already given up just about everything that mattered to her. She was *not* going to walk away from her dearest furry friend. Not if she could help it.

SEVEN

Isaac kept waiting for the other shoe to drop. Daniella was behaving so well during their outing back into DC she worried him. Knowing her the way he thought he did, he kept wondering what kind of stunt she was planning to pull before she eventually escaped from Virginia. And from his protective custody.

He wasn't kidding himself. The pretty nurse was not foolish, nor was she fearless. Somewhere between those two extremes was the real Daniella Dunne.

"I've contacted the patrol that was watching your building," Isaac told her. "They haven't seen any suspicious activity."

"Watching it how?"

"Drive-bys and a few closer inspections. They couldn't afford to put men on it 24/7 since no one was actually hurt there."

"I could have been!"

"Yes, but you weren't. Now, settle down. There's no use getting mad at me. I'm not in charge."

"If I'd been a congressman like Jeffries they'd have guarded my apartment."

"That bomb at his press conference was detonated," Isaac reminded her. One glance told him she was beginning to adjust to hearing discussions of explosives and such. When he'd first met her she'd blanched and looked unsteady every time the subject had come up. Now she was actually chatting about the subject. Sort of.

"True. I don't suppose there's a snowball's chance in July of the two bombs being made by the same person."

His head snapped around. "Why do you ask? Do you think they were?"

"How should I know?" She was studying him intently. "Wait a minute. *You* think they were, don't you? You've suspected him ever since you found out he wasn't in prison anymore."

"I never said that."

"You didn't have to." Daniella's voice rose. "I can see it in your face. What did the lab reports say?"

"I couldn't tell you if I knew."

She slumped back on the passenger seat of the SUV and folded her arms across her chest. "Fine. Don't admit anything. I'll make educated guesses."

"Okay. And while you're at it, maybe you can figure out why your father might have anything to do with wanting to harm a congressman."

Isaac saw her begin to frown before she said, "He wouldn't. Our family came from Florida, as you probably already learned when you checked out my father's arrest record. The only politicians I heard anything about when I was a kid were local, and those changed regularly because they were voted in and out of office."

"I suppose it's possible he taught others how to assemble the devices while he was in prison."

Daniella huffed. "Or they learned from the internet. There's nothing that can't be found on there if you search long enough."

"Unfortunately, you're right." He slowed as they approached her apartment and inclined his head toward it. "Looks peaceful."

"Looks can be deceiving."

"You an expert?"

"Yes. I've learned the hard way that it's best to trust no one."

"You're exaggerating."

Her eyebrows arched. "Am I?"

Pulling parallel with the curb, Isaac stopped the SUV. "Here's what we'll do. You wait while I check the hallway and parking areas with Abby. Then we'll go inside together and let her get a whiff of your place from the doorway."

"And then what?"

Isaac could tell his companion was getting testy but it couldn't be helped. He was there to keep her safe and that's precisely what he intended to do.

"Then we talk it over and decide what our next step will be."

"Meaning, you intend to go first and scare my poor cat again. I can't say I'm thrilled about that."

He'd opened the driver's door and placed one foot on the ground when he heard Abby whine and looked around to see why.

His jaw dropped. "Hey! Where do you think you're going?"

Daniella waved to him over her shoulder. She paused on the sparse lawn. "Hurry up and maybe I won't go in without you."

If he hadn't been hurt he could have easily overtaken her, even if she'd tried to get away. As things stood, however, he figured he'd better comply.

What he wanted was to shout at her for taking even one little step ahead, which, of course, was the direct opposite of the smart thing to do. The more he railed at her, the more likely she was to rebel.

Muttering to himself, Isaac grabbed the end of Abby's leash and joined Daniella, letting the dog lead them both down the hallway.

Abby began to bark before they'd gone all the way. Little wonder. The entrance to the apartment had been smashed in! The wooden jamb was splintered and the door hung half off its hinges.

Someone, somehow, had broken in despite the patrols. And they hadn't been particularly subtle about it.

Daniella gasped. "What? How?"

"Doesn't matter. Just stay back."

She progressed from fear to righteous anger in mere moments. "How *dare* he!"

When she tried to push Isaac aside, she found him immovable. "Get out of my way! I have to go find my cat. He must be terrified."

"That's not our biggest problem." Isaac held on to her forearm and used a tilt of his chin to point to his dog before easing the broken door farther open.

Abby had not only stopped barking, she now sat very still with only her nose twitching, staring directly at the partially obstructed entrance.

"She—she thinks there's a bomb in there?" Daniella knew better than to question the well-trained canine's instincts, yet was having trouble wrapping her mind around reality.

"That would be my conclusion," Isaac said. "I'm not happy she alerted, but I sure am happy you didn't go charging into the place ahead of us and blow yourself up. That would leave a terrible black mark on Abby's spotless record."

Daniella rolled her eyes. "Sarcasm? Now?"

"May as well make fun of a narrow escape instead of letting it paralyze you. You're familiar with that kind of gallows humor in our professions. We've discussed it before."

"Yeah. It's all that keeps us sane sometimes." She gestured at the damaged door. "Well, go get it over with. I want my cat and I'm not leaving here this time until I find him."

Daniella realized that Puddy could have escaped at any time after the break-in but chose to believe that the loud noise, plus whoever may have entered the apartment, would have sent him scampering for cover.

And now? Now it was possible that Isaac and Abby might be seriously hurt—or worse—merely doing their jobs. That thought spurred her to call after them, "Be careful. Both of you."

It was bad enough to believe she'd inadvertently caused her mother's death. She didn't want the responsibility for others on her conscience, too.

She liked Isaac Black. Really liked him. Not only was he amusing and attractive, he loved animals, had a nice family and got along with just about everybody.

Picturing his life brought envy and she immediately quashed it. The man chased down bombs for a living. No matter how much he seemed to have going for him at present, his life was always on the line. Each new day would bring more dangers, more threats, more opportunities for one tiny error to steal all his blessings.

A world without him in it was unthinkable, yet there she stood, imagining that very thing and feeling… Feeling what? Loss? Loneliness? Hopelessness? All those and more. An overwhelming sense of bereavement cloaked her, heart and soul, making her shiver and causing actual physical pain.

Hugging herself, she began rocking and moaning inside, a silent warning trapped behind her closed lips.

It wasn't until Isaac was again standing beside her that she was able to marshal more self-control.

He holstered his weapon and gently touched her arm while the friendly beagle nudged her knees and begged to be petted.

"Are you all right?" he asked, leaning close to speak softly.

"I am if you are."

Intent on hiding her worry and undue personal concern, Daniella figured she'd succeeded. However, the moment she let her gaze meet his and saw the same tender emotional connection reflected there, her confidence began to collapse like a lobbyist's backroom deal.

The final step in the destruction of her will was Isaac's sweet smile. There was something so special, so wonderful about it she could no longer keep her distance.

Without further thought she slid her arms around his neck and stepped into his embrace.

He steadied them both. "Whoa. What's all this?"

"You risked your life for me."

As she felt his arms encircling her and pulling her closer, she heard him say, "In that case, lady, you're way behind. This is the second or third time I've rescued you. You owe me at least one more hug."

That glib comment helped snap her out of her disconcerting tailspin. Leaning away, she gave him a playful smack on the shoulder and grinned. "Oh yeah? Does everybody you protect reward you like this?"

Isaac's broad grin matched hers when he replied, "Nope. Only the damsels in distress."

* * *

"Believe it or not, there was no real bomb. All Abby found was a crumpled paper bag that must have contained explosives at one time. It's empty now."

"You're crazy! Why didn't you call the bomb squad?"

"Because a cat was batting the bag around your bedroom like it was a toy and chewing on it while he shredded it with his back feet. I figured, since it hadn't blown up the kitty, it was not dangerous."

"Puddy? You saw him?"

Chuckling, he released her and followed with Abby, thoroughly enjoying the afternoon now that there was no impending danger. "Fine thing. You cancel my reward hug to go looking for a mangy old cat."

"He's not mangy and he's only middle-aged in cat years."

"Look in the bedroom," Isaac said. "And try to get the bag away from him without touching it too much. I don't expect there to be many clues left but you never know. The lab techs might be able to get traces of something besides cat spit from it."

Daniella dropped to her knees by the bed and lifted the side of the bedspread to peer beneath the box spring. Although she didn't indicate she'd even heard his instructions, she straightened with a big, furry, green-eyed black cat tucked under one arm and the remnants of the crumpled paper bag in the other.

"Is this what you wanted?" She held a ragged edge of the soggy paper between thumb and forefinger.

"That's it. Do you have a new plastic bag I can put it in? Otherwise we'll have to wait for our CSIs—crime scene investigators."

"I know what CSI means. I watch TV."

Isaac had to laugh. Daniella looked as proud as a cat

presenting a dead mouse, and the real cat looked and sounded ready to pounce on poor Abby and tear her to shreds at the first opportunity.

"In the kitchen," she said. "The cabinet to the right of the fridge."

"Gotcha. Be right back." He hesitated and eyed the hissing, growling animal in her arms. "Are you sure you can handle that monster?"

"We'll be fine. Just take the dog with you."

"Gladly."

In less than a minute he had located the correct cupboard and returned to hold out a large storage bag. "Drop it in here and it won't get damaged any more than it already is."

"Sorry about what Puddy did. Are you positive there's nothing else in here that might be dangerous? I mean, suppose they brought a bomb in that bag? It could be anywhere."

"We checked the entire apartment," Isaac assured her, shaking his head for emphasis. "There is no danger, at least not in here. It would probably be a good idea to let Abs go over your car again if you intend to pick it up from the police impound yard."

"Should I? Could I? I hadn't even considered it."

"If that's what you want. However, I think you'll stay safer if you let me continue to chauffeur you for the present. We can't be sure nobody is watching for your car or maybe planted a bug on it, intending to track you down that way. Then again, I had it towed to the storage yard to convince them you'd moved away."

"Good idea. Didn't you say I should stay at your house for the same reason?"

"Maybe. I don't recall."

"You don't recall? Give me a break. You know exactly

what you're doing every second of every day. If you didn't you'd have been killed long ago."

"I think you're giving me too much credit."

"And you're giving me too little! Aargh!"

Her guttural groan of anger and frustration made Isaac jump and startled the anxious cat enough that it wiggled out of her arms. To his surprise, Daniella allowed it to wander off, though she did keep an eye on it.

Giving voice to her emotions must have felt good because she continued making unintelligible grumbling sounds before she finally said, "That's it. I've had it. I'm done."

"Done with what?"

"Being a victim," she said flatly, blowing a noisy sigh. "It's over. I was a scared kid when all this started but I'm not a child anymore. I've built a career and made a comfortable place for myself. No despicable man, father or not, is going to drive me away from the roots I've put down. If Terence Fagan thinks he can scare me off, he has another think coming."

"Whoa. Hold on," Isaac interjected. "It's all well and good to stand up to evil, but you have to be sensible about it. Until we can put him back behind bars, you still need to be careful."

"Fine. I'll report to the marshals and let them help me, but I'm going to make it clear that any relocation they arrange will only be temporary. I love my job here and, believe it or not, I love this city, even if it is full of politicians."

Isaac arched his eyebrows and smiled at her. "Wow. I've never seen this side of you. You really are determined, aren't you?"

When she faced him, hands fisted on her hips, chin

jutting stubbornly and said, "Mister, you have no idea," Isaac realized she had made a major turnaround.

He also knew that irrational bravado could prove fatal unless she tempered it with good sense. In his experience, more than one victim had tried to turn the tables on a stalker and had paid for such foolishness with his or her life. That was not going to happen to Daniella. Not on his watch.

The opportunity to hide her and to give her subtle direction was invaluable. He would not waste his chance to influence her choices, even if he had to enlist the help of his siblings. Both of them had military training and were more than capable of defending themselves, as well as the stubborn nurse. She wouldn't have to be made aware of all their steps to safeguard her. As a matter of fact, the less Daniella knew about the defenses arrayed around her, the better she'd probably behave.

Nodding, Isaac made sure she was looking at him, then inclined his head to direct her attention to the closet. "Okay. Pack the last of the things you can't live without and figure out how we're going to transport your wild cat while I call this in, tell them what you want to do and get my orders."

"Be sure you make it perfectly clear that I am not running away this time. All I'm doing is stepping aside so you and your fellow cops can nab my dad. Understand?"

"Completely."

Leaving Abby with her would have made him happier, but in view of prior experience with the unfriendly cat he decided to keep the beagle at his side, where she'd be safe from feline tooth and claw.

A quick call to his office gave him the private contact number for the witness protection program in that area. The rest would be up to Daniella later.

Setting up an appointment for her to be interviewed at his home was easy. Now his only remaining problem was making sure she listened to the advice of the inspectors. Not all the victims in witness protection did. He knew it took an enormous amount of discipline to blindly follow someone else's plans for your daily existence. He also knew that failing to do so was often treacherous. Even deadly.

Daniella had no idea what Puddy would do riding in the same vehicle as Abby, but she hadn't expected what actually happened.

Their crates were side by side. The cat's was made of plastic with a metal door, meaning Puddy's view of Abby was limited. It didn't seem to matter. Daniella heard a low rumble of displeasure that quickly became a roar rising and falling in a discordant wave of sound.

Isaac chuckled. "Is that your cat? He sounds like he's trying to imitate a lion."

She had to smile back. "I suspect he is. I've heard him growl a little before but nothing like this."

Instead of expressing himself and then quieting, Puddy continued. "Oh, dear," Daniella remarked. "I'm sorry."

"Not as sorry as we're both going to be," Isaac managed to say just as Abby joined in the chorus with a "Yip, yip, yip, owoooo…" that rattled the windows of the air-conditioned SUV.

Clapping her hands over her ears, Daniella glanced at Isaac and grinned. "That's *terrible* harmony. They'll never make it in the music business."

"I knew it was coming," he shouted over the clamor rising from the cargo area. "Abs is a beagle. Howling is one of her favorite pastimes."

"Sounds like it," Daniella yelled back. She let go of

her ears long enough to reach for the radio, intending to see if recorded music would distract the antagonists.

Isaac's yelp stopped her before she was able to do much. He quickly flicked switches, laughing raucously.

To her embarrassment, the car's communication system crackled and someone said, "Unit Five, dispatch. Are you all right out there?"

"Affirmative," Isaac said. "Abby is singing."

"Sounds more like you're both being overrun by a gang of crazed monkeys," the voice countered. "You sure you're okay?"

By this time Daniella's prior nervousness had contributed to her emotional unsteadiness and she was laughing so hard she was weeping and gasping for breath.

"Hush," Isaac warned, chuckling along with her. "They already think I'm in trouble."

"Mister," she managed between giggles and sniffles, "you have no idea."

He smiled back at her, arched his eyebrows and rolled his eyes. "Maybe I didn't before but I'm starting to get the picture—loud and clear."

EIGHT

Time flew by for Daniella. Puddy had finally settled down about being shut in her bedroom and had quit sticking his paw out under the door, where Abby could try to lick it. Once Daniella had realized the little dog meant no harm, she'd opted to let the animals work out their differences with the partition of solid wood between them.

She'd also done all she could to take over some daily chores and hoped her efforts were appreciated. Something in her nature insisted she must earn her way, participate fully, in order to deserve a place in the small family. There were a lot of things she didn't know how to do, such as wield hammer and nails, but she was a wiz with a duster and vacuum, and could even cook, much to Becky's delight.

Intending to wash a few windows to kill time until her afternoon appointment with witness protection, she had located a bucket, sponge and paper towels, and was searching for a stepladder when she heard a car approaching. More than a little anxious, she looked around and saw a dark sedan kicking up dust on the long driveway.

"Oh, dear. Is it that time already?"

She laid aside her cleaning supplies and headed for the den to find Isaac, wanting him present when she spoke with the marshal.

"Isaac?" she called down the hallway, one hand cupped at the side of her mouth. "Isaac! Where are you?"

No answer came. Frustrated, she turned toward the front door, brushed her hands on her jeans, smoothed her hair, checked her image in the hallway mirror, then peeked through the narrow windows flanking the main entrance.

As the dark, unmarked car came to a smooth stop in front of the house, she saw only the driver. He paused for a few seconds, apparently speaking on his radio, then opened his car door and stepped out, squaring a broad-brimmed hat on his head and donning aviator glasses as he did so.

"Isaac!" Daniella's shout echoed in the foyer. "The marshal's here."

Still no answer. She gathered her courage and stood tall. If she was going to be master of her own fate the way she'd vowed, it was time to behave that way. Never mind that she was quaking inside. What mattered was how she presented herself and how well she was able to mask her latent fear. The way she figured it, the more she acted poised and calm and in control, the easier it would be to actually begin to feel that way.

Her hand closed on the brass knob and twisted. The door swung open easily. Daniella took a deep breath and forced a smile for the marshal's benefit.

She stepped outside.

Pulled the heavy wooden door closed.

Turned.

Looked up—and saw the leering grin of her father!

Jake tapped his brother on the shoulder. "Did you hear something?"

"Like what? I can hardly hear myself think when you're running that saw."

"Sorry." Jake flipped the off switch and the table saw

blade began a high-pitched whine, its tone dropping as it slowed.

Isaac strained to hear beyond the barn where he'd been holding up the free ends of two-by-fours so Jake could trim them accurately. He glanced at his watch. "I'd better go check on Daniella. Her appointment with somebody from the marshal's office is in a half hour and I don't want her to be startled if she's lost track of time."

"What, exactly, is going on with you two?"

"Nothing. Why?"

The older brother arched his brows and rolled his eyes. "Yeah, right. Tell me another fairy tale. I've seen the way you treat her."

"I'm just doing my job, that's all."

"Uh-huh. So what's her excuse?"

Frowning, Isaac shook his head. "I don't know what you're talking about."

"Okay. Have it your way." Jake shrugged. "But don't waste your breath denying you've seen her making eyes at you. If the attraction were any plainer she'd be throwing herself at your feet."

"That's ridiculous."

"Ask Becky. She agrees with me. And we're both worried about what you may be getting yourself into. I don't care what you say, it isn't only innocent people who end up in witness protection, you know."

"Look. Daniella saw her mother murdered. All she's guilty of is testifying to the truth."

"So who's after her? You gave us a description of the guy we're supposed to look out for, so you may as well tell us the rest. Becky figures to pry the whole story out of her sooner or later, anyway."

Taking a deep breath and releasing it as a sigh, Isaac conceded. "Her own father. That's why Daniella didn't want to talk about it. She's embarrassed to admit that Terence Fagan is her dad, let alone that he swore to kill her because her testimony put him in prison."

Jacob was nodding. "Wow. Okay. I'll buy that. So what's plan B?"

Walking with his brother toward the rear of the house while still favoring his sore leg, Isaac slowly shook his head. "I have no idea. Once we've conferred with the marshal today and discussed the ramifications of Fagan's early release, we should have some kind of a plan. Daniella says she wants to stop running, but taking a stand right now may not be her smartest move."

He felt his cheeks warm as he thought about a future that included the pretty nurse. Such fantasies were likely to be futile, yet he didn't seem able to stop entertaining them. Whatever happened, however their blossoming relationship ended, he would always remember her fondly and pray that she was happy and well.

In his heart of hearts, he wished there were some way for them to remain in contact, but the moment she was forced back into protective custody the invisible chain that connected them would be broken—unless she chose to return, as she'd claimed she would. He wasn't holding his breath. A lot of things could change in the length of time she might have to be away.

The warm spring air was stirring, the sunlight soothing in spite of the sheen of perspiration on Isaac's brow. He halted and raised his arm to shade his eyes. "What's that?"

"Where?" Jacob was beside him, peering into the distance as his brother pointed.

"There. It looks like a dust cloud."

"I don't see anything."

"Maybe I was imagining it. Or maybe it dissipated.

It was really faint to start with." Nevertheless, he picked up the pace.

"What's the rush?"

"I don't know," Isaac admitted. "I just have a funny feeling."

"Funny ha-ha or funny peculiar?"

"Funny risky and dangerous."

"I'll come with you."

"No." The seriousness of the order was unmistakable. "It's probably the marshal. You stay outside. Shut the dogs in the barn so they don't get in the way, then keep watch, just in case. I'm going to pick up my duty weapon and find Daniella."

Isaac climbed the wooden porch steps and slowly eased open the back door. In several more limping strides he was standing in the enormous farm kitchen.

By looking down the main-floor hallway he could see through a multipaned window in the room that had been a parlor when the house was new.

Daniella stood just outside. She was fine. His breath whooshed out with relief and he smiled, nevertheless making a quick detour to the den to pick up his firearm, as planned.

In less than a minute he was in the parlor/living room. It was plain Daniella was upset, but she seemed in control of her basic emotions. He focused past her to the typical dark, unmarked car parked in the driveway. Although he couldn't see him, he figured the marshal had arrived early and caught her by surprise. That would explain her anxiety.

Since the urgency of his earlier worries had abated, Isaac slowed his pace and favored his injury as he crossed the room. It seemed the most natural thing in the world to keep watching Daniella as he walked.

Her back was partially to him so he wasn't able to see her face. Her shoulders were back, her spine straight and she was gesturing with her hands as if expressing herself forcefully.

Isaac froze midstride, put too much weight on his sore leg and faltered. Something had just changed. Something was wrong. Very wrong. Daniella had raised both hands as if surrendering and she were backing away from whoever she'd been talking to.

A man's hand shot out. Grabbed one of her wrists. Yanked her out of Isaac's view.

He threw open the front door and stepped through, his gun at the ready, in time to see her being forced down the stairs toward the black car.

Senses reeling, he realized he was looking at a marshal's car, uniform shirt and standard-issue hat—over faded jeans and dirty running shoes. This man was an imposter!

"Stop or I'll shoot!" Isaac yelled, taking a marksman's stance.

Daniella's captor laughed rawly. "No, you won't. You might hit the girl." He pressed the barrel of a revolver to her temple. "Or this gun might accidentally go off."

"What do you want?"

The fake lawman's grin radiated evil. "Her. But not for long," he said. "I just need to teach her a lesson."

It had occurred to Isaac the moment he'd seen the attacker that he might be Terence Fagan, although it was hard to tell for sure with the hat brim shading most of his face and silvered sunglasses masking his eyes.

"You're Fagan."

"Give the man a medal. He wins the prize."

"Listen, this is crazy," Isaac told him. "You got out of jail legally. Don't put yourself back in just to get revenge."

While the captor continued edging closer to the car, Isaac kept pace, narrowing the distance slightly with each step. The way he figured, Fagan would have to open the door to shove Daniella in before he could get behind the wheel. That should be enough time to launch a counter-attack and free her.

And if it wasn't?

Isaac refused to even consider failure as an option.

He just hoped he could survive whatever personal sacrifice he'd have to make in order to bring her through unscathed.

Daniella wanted to do serious damage to the despicable man who was trying to kidnap her. Thrashing, she kicked behind, stomped on the tops of his feet, threw her weight from side to side. Nothing loosened his grip.

"Let me go!" she screeched at the top of her lungs. "Let me go, you dirty…"

Fagan did let her arm go in order to backhand her across the face before she could finish. The blow sent her flying. The instant her hands and knees hit the dirt, she began to scramble away.

Terence Fagan cursed.

Isaac leaped at him as best he could, not even feeling the stitches in his calf. They slammed into the side of the car and went down together.

Isaac's free hand grasped the wrist of his adversary to divert the lethal weapon.

Fagan did the same to him and also began to kick, landing a solid blow to Isaac's leg and causing him to shout in anguish.

Instead of running for her life, Daniella circled the car and leaped onto her father's back, wrapping both arms around his neck and trying to choke him to get him to release Isaac.

In a flurry of arms and legs, screeching and groaning, the three rolled over and over on the ground.

In the background, Isaac heard his brother's shout and a cacophony of barking.

Jacob ran around the corner of the house on the heels of Abby and the enormous mixed-breed farm dogs. He was swinging a shovel like a baseball bat.

Fagan took one look at the slavering, growling canines and screamed, then let go of his gun and everything else, jumped to his feet and dived in the driver's door, scraping Daniella off in the process.

The engine roared. Spinning tires threw a rooster tail of dust and gravel. The big car fishtailed, then straightened and sped away.

"Abby, come. Heel!" Isaac shouted, afraid for the K-9's safety.

The little beagle slid to a halt and the larger dogs did the same, following her back to the yard at a brisk trot, tails waving and looking terribly pleased with themselves.

The sight of Daniella, sitting there in the dirt with her cheeks tearstained and her breathing ragged, tore at Isaac's heart. He reached for her.

She mirrored his actions. In seconds she was in his arms, cradled against his chest, trembling.

He pulled her tighter. Soothed her with murmurs. Wished he'd been there for her when she'd been attacked.

"I'm so sorry," he said softly.

She drew a stuttering breath. "I'm the one who's sorry. I should have recognized my father, even in disguise. Are you hurt? I saw him kicking you."

"It's nothing." He was loath to release her long enough to get to his feet, assuming he could.

When Jacob offered a hand, Isaac took it, pulling Daniella up beside him.

That didn't break them apart. If anything, it strengthened their embrace.

"Is he gone?" Isaac asked his brother.

Jake nodded. "Yeah. Last I saw of him he was turning onto the road and flooring it."

"Terrific."

Keeping one arm firmly around Daniella's waist, Isaac fisted his cell phone and reported the foiled attack, starting with the general direction the fleeing fugitive was headed.

"It was an official car so it shouldn't be hard to locate now that we know Fagan stole it. The uniform, too."

"He—he bragged about killing the real marshal," Daniella added softly, as if loath to say it.

Isaac relayed her information. "Yeah, it's possible. We didn't see any sign of him. His handlers can probably track his movements before he was due here and locate him, hopefully still alive. Tell them I'm sorry I didn't get a chance to examine the car's trunk." He paused to listen. "Okay. Keep us informed."

"What are they going to do?" Daniella asked as soon as the call ended.

"Coordinate a search for the marshal and his car. That has to come first. Then somebody will probably come by here to take our statements. What I can't understand is how Fagan found out when your appointment with the marshal was and how he managed to outwit a professional lawman."

"He told me he put a bug in my apartment and listened to your call to set things up," Daniella explained.

"I should have anticipated that."

Isaac felt her arms tighten slightly, as if imparting moral support, before she said, "Don't beat yourself up about it. There's no way anybody would have suspected what he was up to this time. He's always used indirect action before."

"True. This face-to-face attack changes everything. You realize that, don't you?"

"I do. But I've decided to tell the marshals I'd prefer to handle my relocation myself. The more people who know where I've gone, the bigger the chances of a leak. I don't want innocent people to die because of me."

Isaac didn't totally agree with her logic but decided to save his arguments for later, after she'd calmed down.

It was beginning to look as if destiny had not brought the perfect woman into his life so he could keep her forever, after all. She was going to have to leave DC ASAP, and it would be more than selfish of him to try to hang on to her.

It might even be lethal.

NINE

To Daniella's relief, Isaac got a call that the injured marshal had been located, hospitalized and was expected to recover.

On the negative side, there had been no sightings of Terence Fagan or the stolen car. She and the Black brothers had given official statements about the attack, but in spite of extensive roadblocks and all-points bulletins, Fagan was still on the run.

She had redressed Isaac's injury after the altercation and had found herself actually feeling his pain. As an ER nurse, she had often done the exact same task, yet this had been the first time she'd winced while tending to a patient. Not only had that reaction been a surprise, it had been unnerving to share such strong empathy with the K-9 officer.

Dinner conversation that evening and the next was subdued, for which she was doubly thankful since she felt so guilty about bringing trouble to such a nice family.

It was Becky who broke the charged silence around the table by asking, "So, Daniella…or should we call you something else?"

Eyes lowered while she pushed peas around her plate with a fork, she shrugged. "I suppose you could call me

Ella if you wanted to, but I really prefer Daniella." Unshed tears filled her eyes and she hoped she could hold them back long enough to politely excuse herself and leave the room.

"Daniella it is, then. Why didn't you fill us in about your past when you first arrived? It would have made a lot more sense if we'd known the circumstances."

"It's not your problem. It's mine. Nobody was supposed to know I was here and I didn't want any of you to be involved if I could help it." She glanced up at Isaac. "Didn't you tell them anything?"

"Enough to keep them from getting hurt and help them look out for you if need be," he replied. "I thought the background-story details were yours to provide if you chose. They knew he was middle-aged and I showed them booking photos."

"He looks much older now, doesn't he?" Daniella asked. "Being in prison really aged him."

"It tends to do that." Isaac looked to his sister. "I should have asked earlier. Did you renew your concealed-carry permit?"

"Yes," Becky answered. "I don't use it inside the beltway but since the trouble started I've decided it would be prudent to be armed when I'm at work, particularly if I'm out showing homes to prospective buyers." She looked to their elder brother. "How about you, Jake?"

He grinned. "Hey, I got enough of that when I was deployed overseas. As long as I have my trusty shovel and these two hands, I'll be fine."

Becky rolled her eyes. "You'd better convince him otherwise, Isaac. You're the one with the badge."

"Ha! Since when does he listen to my advice?"

Daniella reached out, laid a hand lightly on Jacob's forearm and said, "Please? I don't want anybody else to get hurt because of me. There's no telling what my father will try before the marshals either give me the okay to leave or insist on putting me somewhere else themselves."

His grin widened and he winked at his siblings. "Well, since you put it that way, I guess I could load the shotgun."

What a relief. "Thank you."

As soon as she looked away from Jacob and made eye contact with Isaac, she noticed that he seemed out of sorts. Given his concern for his family's safety, she found that off-putting attitude a bit puzzling, particularly since his brother had just agreed to take his good advice, thanks to her.

Becky began to giggle, further confusing matters. When Isaac rose from the table without excusing himself first and stalked from the room, both the remaining siblings laughed.

Counting to ten to make sure she wasn't overreacting, Daniella asked, "What's so funny?"

Becky was wiping away happy tears. "It's a private joke."

"Are you sure? It felt a lot like you were laughing at me and my story. Believe me, nothing about it is the least bit amusing." She shivered. "I still think I see shadows of attackers lurking behind every bush and tree."

"We're not laughing at you," Becky said. "Isaac's the one who's funny. He insists he's not interested in you but he's so jealous of poor Jake it's comical."

"Jealous? That's terrible."

"I wouldn't go quite that far," her hostess said. "Our brother may be too focused on his job and Abby a lot of the time, but he's really a nice guy once you get to know him."

Sorrowful, Daniella shook her head. "That's the worst

part of the problem. I can't think of any job that scares me more than his does. Even if I wasn't about to temporarily relocate I'd never consider dating him, let alone getting serious."

"Really?" Becky leaned forward with her elbows on the table. "I think he's very brave."

"Oh, I don't doubt he is," Daniella replied. "But he goes looking for explosives. On purpose. Every day. The gash in his leg is just one example of an assignment gone wrong. Imagine how badly he'd have been hurt if he'd been closer or leaning over it to get a better look." She shivered. "I can still picture every horrible detail of my mother's death. The whole concept of going looking for bombs gives me goose bumps and makes me queasy."

"Then it's probably for the best that you're going to move on," the other woman said. "Tell you what. I'll add you to my prayer list."

"Don't bother. God gave up on me a long time ago."

"You can't really believe that."

Daniella was nodding. "Oh, yes, I do. My mother had strong faith and she still died, even after I prayed and prayed for her."

"That doesn't mean the Lord ignored you. It's possible it was her time to go home to Him. Think about it. You say she was unhappy and stuck in a bad marriage. Her death not only freed her, it gave you a new life, too, and eliminated the cause of her pain."

"But not the cause of mine," Daniella countered. "Terence Fagan is still around, still after me."

"For now," Becky said gently. "Maybe meeting Isaac and the rest of us is God's way of bringing your father's reign of terror to an end, once and for all."

"Humph. I'll believe that when I see it."

Becky smiled so sweetly it was unnerving when she said, "I pray that we'll all see it before something takes you away from us."

The official K-9 unit vehicles Isaac had been expecting rolled up shortly before the sun set that evening. He had already shut his farm dogs in the barn but Abby was loose because she was familiar with the visitors and highly trained.

He greeted the men, one blond, one darker, with a smile and handshake, then gestured toward the ornate Victorian-style covered front porch, where Daniella waited.

"Adam, Chase, I'd like you to meet Daniella Dunne, aka Ella Fagan. She's the reason I asked you both to stop by with your dogs after work."

Each man nodded politely to Daniella, then they fastened leashes on their canine partners and commanded them to jump down from the areas designed to protect them.

"The Doberman is Ace. His specialty is protection," Isaac said, pointing to Adam and the sleek black-and-brown canine by his side. "The fawn-colored shepherd type with the longer hair and black mask is a Belgian Malinois named Valor. He's trained mostly for search and rescue but both are cross-trained to track suspects and protect their handlers if necessary."

One hand resting on the wooden railing, Daniella descended partway to the yard. "They're beautiful animals." She looked to Isaac. "But why are they here tonight?"

"For added insurance," he replied. "I want them to do another sweep of the property, just in case." Although he'd been trying to broach the subject with nonchalance, it was immediately clear to him that Daniella was not fooled.

"You sensed something was wrong, too? I wasn't my imagination playing tricks on me?"

Isaac was quick to reassure her. "No. I didn't sense anything and I haven't seen a sign of your father, but I did overhear you telling Becky and Jake you were jumping at shadows."

"I thought you'd left before I said that."

"I try to never get too far from you, especially lately," Isaac admitted. "Think of this search tonight the way you do preventive medicine. It's sensible to head off problems, if you can, before you get sick. Right?"

She nodded and folded her arms across her chest, hugging herself as if the spring breeze suddenly carried a chill.

Watching her gaze dart from man to man, ending with him, Isaac smiled slightly and asked, "You can see the logic in that, can't you?"

Her lips pressed together. She squinted. "I can see a lot of things, not the least of which is how worried you are. What are you not telling me?"

"Nothing." He drew an imaginary X over his heart with one finger. "Honest."

"Assuming I buy that," Daniella drawled, "why does this look like an off-duty favor instead of a regular assignment?"

"Because it is." He was unwilling to lie, even if the truth did make her more paranoid. "You met our boss, Captain McCord, at the hospital when I was being treated. His job is a tough one, particularly considering the amount of territory our unit is responsible for, including the White House. He didn't feel that another check on this farm was necessary so he left it up to me to recruit a few volunteers if I wanted it done."

Isaac watched Adam give her a wave and Chase a two-fingered casual salute.

"I want you to split up," he told his comrades, pointing. "Adam and Ace can cover the east side of the house. Chase and Valor can take the west. Abby and I will join you in the backyard and work both sides from the middle. Ready?"

Before giving the signal to begin, he shot a stern look at Daniella. "You wait in the house." He could tell how close she was to arguing and then saw when she made the decision to comply.

"All right. This is your farm, your family and your friends, so I'll do things your way. This time." Her gaze passed over the men and animals. "Please, please be careful. I know Terence Fagan all too well. He's apt to try anything."

"That's why I'm including myself and Abby," Isaac said. "We know what we're doing."

"Remind yourself of that every time the gash in your leg starts to throb," Daniella snapped back. "You may be crazy-brave, but you're not bulletproof."

The blonder of the two other men clapped him on the shoulder and grinned. "No kidding. Some of us have been thinking of taking up a collection to buy you a head-to-toe set of body armor like the guys in the bomb squad wear." He eyed the leg Isaac was favoring. "What do you say, buddy?"

Chuckling, Isaac batted his hand away. "Let's just concentrate on doing a good sweep, shall we? Becky's out on a date but she left coffee and cake waiting for us in the kitchen."

"Well, why didn't you say so? Let's get at it."

The joking around was a common coping mechanism and usually worked to relieve tension. The moment Isaac looked back, however, his smile disappeared.

Daniella had one arm wrapped around a porch post and was leaning against it as if she needed the added support merely to stay on her feet. Her eyes glistened. Wind ruffled her honey-colored hair that seemed to be getting lighter by the day. The jeans Becky had loaned her had never looked better on anyone, either.

Rays of the setting sun behind Daniella made her fairly glow and seem almost ethereal. For a brief moment he saw her, not as she was, but as he dreamed she could be. Innocent. Unencumbered. Free. Eager to embrace the joys of life, perhaps with him.

Then, his mind cleared and he snapped back to reality.

There was nothing about Daniella that fit his life plan. She was tortured by her past. Threatened by her present. And only half likely to have a future.

It was that future he must defend. With or without a place for himself in it, he had to make sure she had one.

The seconds and minutes dragged by for Daniella. She'd managed to keep one or more of the K-9 cops in sight by moving from window to window inside the old house.

Her final attempt led her to climb to the second floor and peer out her bedroom window so she could see over the barn roof and into the plowed fields beyond. An added comfort was the purring coming from Puddy as she cradled him and gently stroked his long fur.

The dogs and their handlers seemed to be pacing themselves and carefully moving ahead. Abby's nose remained close to the ground while the other two alternated between scents in the air or the soil. It was fascinating to watch, almost soporific, given their methodical back-and-forth movements.

Isaac had had her car checked for bugs, then moved from police impound. He'd stored it under a tarp in his barn rather than disposed of it before they knew what the marshals' plans were.

Not that I care, she mused, slightly disgusted that she hadn't been able to convince herself to simply hop into it and drive away. Part of her wanted to flee while her more sensible side insisted she wait for all the red tape to be finished properly. Logic won. Barely.

A slight movement off to the side in a grove of maples caught her attention. It had been more of a sense than actual sight; a feeling that something had shifted in her usually well-ordered universe. Had it? Or was her fertile imagination merely taking her on another unwanted journey?

Concentrating, she noted that the winged seeds on the tree were shimmering in the evening light. A few were even breaking loose to swirl to the ground like helicopter blades.

Her hand had stilled. The cat nudged her fingers with his head in a plea for more affection.

Although Daniella looked away for only a second, when her focus returned to the base of the trees she realized something had changed. But what?

This scenario reminded her of those puzzles where minor things are different in similar pictures and the viewer is challenged to figure out what has been altered.

Trees, leaves, seeds, shadows. All seemed identical to her earlier observations.

Then, she saw it. An instant of flash. Sunlight on metal or glass. A gun? Binoculars? Maybe a telescopic sight on a rifle?

It didn't matter. Whoever was down there was now behind the men who were searching the farm fields. When they retraced their steps they'd walk right into an ambush!

The cat wiggled free and scooted under the bed, obviously sensing her tension.

Trembling all over, Daniella let him go his way without a second thought. Part of her brain was screaming *Go! Help them.*

Contradicting orders mingled with her desire for bravery and she pictured herself shinnying under the bed beside her frightened cat.

What should she do? What *could* she do? Becky had gone out for the evening, presumably taking her handgun, and all Jake had to protect himself was that stupid shovel and a shotgun. A lot of good those would do him against a rifle, particularly at a distance.

No. She couldn't enlist aid. She had to handle this situation herself. After all, the prowler was most likely after her. She'd brought the danger here and it was up to her to warn the K-9 officers. *But how?*

Her first thought was to throw open the window and shout at them, until she realized that that would bring them on the run, right into the waiting trap.

"Can I run fast enough to keep from getting shot?" she murmured to herself.

Pressing her lips together, she shook her head. "Not a chance." She'd be doing well to even clear the back porch, let alone make it around the big barn and across the field before being spotted and stopped.

What choices are left?

No easy answers came to her. The sensible thing might be for her to drive Isaac's SUV or maybe Jacob's pickup truck, but first she'd have to lay her hands on the right set of keys. Isaac probably had his with him and if she asked Jake for the truck keys she'd have to tell him why she wanted them, meaning he was bound to interfere, perhaps fatally.

That left only one option. The car in the barn under the tarp. Daniella gritted her teeth and clenched her jaw. That car was where her father had left the bomb for her. Had he been on the premises long enough to have had a chance to repeat his attempt? Isaac had checked, of course, but that didn't mean that someone else couldn't have tampered with her car. She rooted through her purse searching for her spare keys. Where were they? They had to be in there.

Just as she was about to give up, her fingers touched the familiar ring. Fisting it, Daniella ran for the stairs and descended so fast she almost missed a step and fell.

Her pulse sped. Her breathing was shallow. Her knees threatened to fold and drop her to the floor before she accomplished her goal. She would not let that happen. Lives hung in the balance.

Centrifugal force carried her around the newel post at the bottom and headed her in the right direction. There was no time to search for protection or develop a disguise. Besides, the less encumbered she was, the faster she could move.

The element of surprise would be her armor. Dashing through the kitchen, she yanked open the back door and sailed off the end of the porch, not bothering to take the stairs.

Landing was trickier. Momentum pitched her forward. She caught herself on her hands and pushed off like a sprinter, without missing a beat.

The big barn door was closed so she headed for the

smaller one at the side farthest from the maple trees that hid her enemy.

In the seconds it took her to work the latch, she kept expecting to hear the crack of a shot and feel its impact.

Instead, she was bowled over by three dogs the size of ponies. Barking and howling, they crowded out the open door and took off around the barn as if their tails were on fire. Would their arrival be enough of a warning? Or would they cause the officers to race back to the house without any thought for themselves? Probably the latter. Unless she acted swiftly.

Daniella paused to take stock. Several cats had made themselves at home atop the tarp covering her car. She shooed them away and whipped it off, then pivoted to free the crude latch holding the larger doors closed.

They swung partially out of the way while Daniella slid behind the wheel, hoping, praying her father had not discovered this vehicle and tampered with it again.

She missed the key slot twice, then grabbed her trembling wrist with her other hand to steady it. The key turned easily. The engine groaned, stuttered, quit! *And the car did not blow up! Praise God!*

Again she hit the ignition. Stomped on the gas pedal. Dropped the transmission into Drive. With a grinding of gears and squealing of tires, the car shot toward the doors.

They hadn't opened fully when she'd released them, but Daniella didn't care. She missed the left one, clipped the edge of the right and spun her car in a half circle, throwing a rooster tail of dust and dirt higher than the top of the car.

Her fingers felt like part of the wheel with her mind directing the engine, her feet urging it on. Nothing could distract her now. Not even being shot at.

The car fishtailed around the corner of the barn and

straightened out, heading directly toward the plowed field the K-9 officers were searching.

Shock reflected off Isaac's face, his jaw dropped and he began to wave his arms at her.

Daniella belatedly realized why he had been signaling so frantically. Her hood and front fenders plowed through a barbed-wire fence, snapping the spans and whipping long lengths of spiked, twisted wire behind her.

Her front and rear windows shattered simultaneously, and Daniella let out a piercing scream. Only the windshield stayed together, its surface a tangle of spidery cracks. She hit the brakes, skidded sideways and came to a halt mere feet from the men and all the dogs.

Someone jerked her door open and dragged her from the car. When she landed on the uncomfortable ridges of plowed dirt, she expected to be welcomed.

"You almost killed us!" Isaac roared.

Daniella shook her head and waved away the clouds of dust with both hands, blinking to clear her vision. "I did nothing of the kind. I just saved your lives."

"By whipping us with wire and running us over?"

"No. By keeping you from walking into an ambush when you came back to the house to see why your other dogs were out. I saw somebody hiding under one of the maple trees below my room."

"Did anybody else see this person?"

"No, but...I know there was someone there. I saw a glint of light reflecting off metal or glass. I know I did. I thought it was a gun."

"Right."

She saw one of the other officers tap Isaac on the shoulder and gesture at her car. He stepped closer in spite of the loose fencing wire that was still festooning the hood.

When he turned to look back at her, his anger was gone. So was the color in his face. All he did was point.

Joining him, she understood. It had not been the collision with the fence that had caused her windows to shatter.

A hole as big around as her little finger was punched through the fractured safety glass.

A hole the size of a bullet.

TEN

Isaac kept hold of Abby's leash and slipped an arm around Daniella's shoulders. By unspoken agreement, Adam radioed headquarters, Chase called the local police and Isaac used his cell to notify Jacob.

"Hi, Jake."

"What in the world is going on? I thought I heard a shot."

"You did. Stay inside. Somebody's using us for target practice. Nobody's hurt so far. If you keep your head down, it should stay that way."

"Where are you?"

"Behind the barn. You probably can't see us from the house. Just don't let yourself be silhouetted in the windows, whatever you do."

"Is it Fagan?"

"Can't tell," Isaac said, reluctant to say much in front of the trembling woman in his arms. "Might be."

"Okay. I'll go warn Daniella."

The chuckle Isaac managed sounded more like a cough. "Um, that won't be necessary. She's here with me."

"Outside? Is she *nuts*?"

"Maybe. Probably. The important thing is that you stay

out of sight until the cops arrive and you warn Becky to check with one of us before driving home."

"Right. Will do." There was a pause. "You *are* going to tell me exactly what's going on when you come in. I don't care if your girlfriend is embarrassed about her family. I want all the details. Copy?"

"You already know most of them," Isaac argued, "but all right. We'll answer any questions. I promise. Now call Becky for me, will you? My battery's low and I want to save it for emergencies."

Ending the call, he turned his full concentration on the woman at his side and scowled. "Do you have a death wish?"

"Of course not." She leaned away and met his gaze boldly. "I have a life wish, for myself and everybody else I know. If you guys had started back to the house, the sniper would have had clear shots at all of you. I spotted him, but you had no idea of the danger, so I did what I had to do."

"You've never heard of phones?"

He saw her eyebrows draw together in a clear frown. "Yes," she drawled, "but somebody took mine away and never replaced it. I knew if I asked Jake to call you he'd make me stay in the house and put himself in danger. It wasn't his job, it was mine. I brought the problem with me and I intend to face it—as many times as necessary."

"You'd better hope nobody ever gives you a professional psych eval, lady. You sound certifiable."

"Don't raise your voice to me."

"I wasn't, I…" Isaac realized she was right. He had been yelling. Little wonder. Once again Daniella had had a narrow escape and his racing heart hadn't yet recovered. Matter of fact, the more she revealed about her convoluted reasoning, the more concerned he became.

He lightly touched her hand. "Look. I'm sorry. I was reacting to what you'd done and it scared me to death. You may have escaped in the past but that's no guarantee you won't be injured, or worse, if you keep on defying your father."

"I'm as smart as he is."

"Yes, but he's also crafty. You can't expect him to behave rationally. His warped mind won't let him."

"Because he's a sociopath. I know," Daniella admitted. "I spent a lot of time studying about people like him in the hopes I could understand him. He truly believes he's in the right and is allowed to act in any manner that brings him to his goals, no matter who gets hurt in the process."

"Exactly. That was the conclusion of the prison psychiatrist, too. Fagan won't listen to reason because he thinks he's infallible. And he sees you as a roadblock to the perfect life he envisions."

A small smile twitched at the corners of her mouth, taking Isaac by surprise.

"I am a roadblock," Daniella said, speaking softly. "If I'm the only one who can get that awful man off the streets and back into jail, then I'll do whatever I have to do to make it happen."

Left unsaid was the part of her vow that knifed into his gut, his heart, and left him feeling real pain. She meant, if she had to die as her mother had in order to see justice done, she'd willingly make that sacrifice.

Yes, it was brave. It was also foolhardy. There was a big difference between the work he did for law enforcement and her idea that only she could stop Fagan.

If he didn't accomplish anything else while they were together, Isaac vowed he was going to teach her that. Or die trying.

* * *

They remained crouched behind Daniella's car, just in case, until they heard sirens and saw flashing red-and-blue lights approaching the house. The officers in the patrol cars slid to stops in the front and rear of the old Victorian, panned the scene with spotlights, then cautiously disembarked, guns drawn.

Isaac stood, causing Daniella to do the same. Or try to. His hand on her shoulder shoved her back down, and she didn't like that treatment one bit. "Hey. Let go."

"Keep your head down until I say you can stand."

"Why? Is your head bulletproof?"

The look he shot her was so disparaging—and so silly looking—she almost laughed. Tension often did that to her. Truth be told, she'd lots rather get the giggles than burst into tears every time she was challenged or felt in jeopardy. That particular thought did make her smile. "I'll take sniper avoidance for a thousand, Alex," she murmured, earning another scathing look from Isaac.

She busied herself petting Abby until Isaac finally gave her permission to rise.

Dusting off her hands and her jeans, she fell into step behind the men and their working dogs while the farm dogs ran circles around the group and barked excitedly. At a whistle from Jake, they headed for the yard and disappeared, presumably confined in the barn again.

Although she continued to stand back a little ways, Daniella made sure to stay close to a refuge such as the barn or the house or a police car so she'd be ready to duck if anybody located the shooter. Instinct told her the man was long gone, but since she didn't want any more safety-protocol lectures from her host, she figured it would be best to voluntarily keep a low profile.

Listening to the K-9 officers reporting the details of

the attack reminded her of the Spartan way doctors and nurses kept patient records. Impressions and feelings were unimportant in that context but facts were crucial. The trouble was, they had few to go on in this case.

In retrospect she kind of wished she'd waited a little longer to make a break for it in the hopes she'd have gotten more information about the menace waiting in the trees.

Then again, once Isaac and his friends had started back to the house, she'd have lost sight of them until they'd rounded the barn and by that time they'd have been in the shooter's sights.

Daniella shivered and looked toward Isaac. How special he was. How kind. How attractive. How…perfect.

"Yeah," she muttered, huffing derisively at her own idiocy. "Perfect for somebody else maybe."

He glanced over his shoulder. "Did you want to add something? You spotted the perp first."

"No need." She shrugged and slipped her hands into her jeans pockets so he wouldn't see her fingers trembling. "You guys have covered it. I thought the farm dogs might chase him off when they got out past me but apparently not, since there's a hole in my car."

"If you thought that, why did you risk driving out back?"

"Because I couldn't be sure. I figured you'd take one look at them and come looking to see if I was in trouble. If you had, he'd have been able to pick you off like fish in a barrel."

There was no need for her to wonder if her statement had been nonchalant enough because Isaac's scowl deepened noticeably. *Good.* That meant he would be less likely to realize how scared she really was and coddle her.

How she had managed to do what she'd done without being wounded was beyond comprehension. Isaac had been totally right to yell at her for taking such risks. Given a second chance, she strongly doubted she'd be able to convince herself to repeat the same act, let alone do anything when she knew for sure that the prowler was so well armed.

Basically, she was scared witless. "With *witless* being the operative word," she told herself, remembering how sensible her plan had seemed until now, when she could look back on it.

Edging closer to the others, she admitted needing their support, the comfort of their strength, particularly Isaac's. If he decided to put his arm around her shoulders again she was definitely going to leave it there—for as long as possible.

Adrenaline kept Daniella awake and alert for the next hour or so, then dropped her like a deflating helium balloon. The harder she tried to think up excuses for charging out to the barn and driving her car through a fence, the less she agreed that those actions were wise or necessary.

Back in the kitchen with the K-9 officers and the Blacks, she wrapped her hands around a mug of steaming coffee and faced them. Adam and Chase seemed to have accepted her excuses because their postures were relaxed. Conversely, it was clear that Isaac and his brother had not. They were both edgy and staring at her as if she had committed an unpardonable sin.

"Look," she said, trying again. "I wasn't being careless. I simply didn't see another option that would keep everybody safe."

"What about *you*?" Isaac demanded, his words clipped, his expression accusing her of not thinking at all, let alone making a sensible decision.

Daniella leaned back in her chair and yawned, covering her mouth with one hand. "I started this. I'll finish it."

"You did not!" Isaac started to jump to his feet but Jacob and Adam, one seated on either side, stopped him.

"I think what my brother is trying to say," Jake offered, "is that whatever your relatives did or didn't do, you can't be held responsible."

"Terence Fagan is my father. I testified against him. Of course I'm responsible."

"Who says?"

Her attention swung back to Isaac to answer, "I do."

"You're wrong," he told her, sounding less angry and far more downhearted than before. "That man may have destroyed your mother with a bomb, but she wasn't the only one harmed. You were scarred, too. Deeply. And the only way I know of to help you is to remind you that we're all children of God. All of us are guilty to some extent and all are promised forgiveness. We just have to genuinely ask for it and have faith."

She clenched her jaw muscles and sat up straighter in her chair as if prepping to do battle. "Mom took me to church and Sunday school. I know the rules. I also know I will never be able to forgive that man. Never. He took everything from me. My mother. My sense of family. My home and friends. All of it's gone."

"Then maybe the secret is forgiving yourself first," Isaac proposed.

Speechless to learn that he was so close to understanding her internal struggles, Daniella pushed back from the table and rose.

"Leave your plates and cups in the sink, gentlemen," she said. "I'm too tired to wash up now so I'll do the cleanup tomorrow. Good night."

She made it to the sink without rattling her dishes, then

walked stiffly out of the room and began to climb the stairs. Memories of all her earthly father's sins swirled through her mind. It didn't matter what anyone else did or didn't do. She knew whose daughter she was—would always be. Some things were set in stone, like the Ten Commandments, and not subject to change no matter how much she wished they were.

So what about God? she asked herself. There had been a time when she had truly believed she was His child, too. Could Isaac be right? Did she really need to forgive herself the way he'd said?

She clenched her jaw so tightly her cheeks ached. It would take an extraordinary amount of faith to accomplish that, let alone to stop hating the man who had murdered her mother. She not only knew she didn't have the strength for that, but she also wondered if, given the means and opportunity, she would actually consider carrying out the fantasy of retribution by ending his life.

The shock of realizing that doing so would make her just as evil as her father shook her to the core. She paused at the top of the stairs, her hand on the banister, her feet rooted to the floor, and closed her eyes.

Tears slid down her cheeks unheeded. "Please, God," she whispered, "help me. I don't want to be like him."

It was a simple prayer. A child's prayer. And so heartfelt that no other words seemed necessary.

Standing there in the dimly lit hallway, Daniella was astounded to sense divine peace flowing over and around her as if wrapping her in a warm blanket of love.

As she proceeded slowly to her room, she murmured the only thing that felt appropriate. She said, "Thank You, Lord."

* * *

It had taken Isaac and the others another hour of spec-
ulative conversation before they were satisfied they had
done all they could for the present. He had bid his co-
workers good-night and was watching them drive away
when Becky got home.

She parked in front so the porch light would illumi-
nate her way and rolled down her window. "Is it safe to
leave my car?"

Isaac nodded. "Yes. Police canvassed the place and
so did tracking dogs, until that trail went cold. Whoever
was causing trouble before is long gone, at least for the
present, but we'll keep an eye out."

"Jake phoned and told me to make myself scarce. I
would have come home to help you defend the fort if I'd
thought it would help."

"You did the right thing by staying away," Isaac told
her as he opened and held the car door for her. "Having
Daniella playing cavalry was bad enough. The prowler
put a bullet through her car—while she was in it."

"You didn't catch him?"

"No. I doubt we were even close by the time we got
organized. My team's dogs tracked him as far as Judson
Mill Road but lost the trail there. We assume he had a
car waiting."

Becky was through the front door and shedding her
light jacket by the time he finished explaining. "One
shooter or more?" she asked.

"Can't tell. I'm guessing one, judging by the boot
prints under the trees where Daniella first spotted him.
It happened at dusk and was really too dark to tell a whole
lot without setting up crime scene lighting."

"Why didn't you?"

"Because I didn't want to call more attention to the incident. The last thing we need is a bunch of reporters nosing around out here."

"What harm will it do?" his sister asked, arching her eyebrows at him. "If the assailant was Fagan, like we all think, he already knows where his daughter is."

"True. But there's an outside chance it wasn't him."

"Do you really believe that?"

Chagrined, Isaac shook his head and pressed his lips into a thin line. "No." He looked around to make sure they were alone before he added, "I think it was him and he fully intended to kill her."

ELEVEN

One thing was clear in Daniella's mind in the early-morning hours of the following day. She had to leave the farm, one way or another. If the marshals wouldn't give her an official release in a timely fashion, she'd have to take matters into her own hands. The biggest question was, where would she go? And what would she use to support herself until she got another job?

In the past, government agents had taken care of everything, from selling her meager possessions to giving her a small stipend and helping her finish school.

There had been a lump-sum insurance settlement from her mother's estate, too, but she hadn't been able to convince herself to touch it because of what it represented. Perhaps now was the time. All she had to do was figure out how to ditch Isaac long enough to go to the bank and get the money so he wouldn't try to stop her or talk her out of preparing to leave DC.

There was only one person in the house whom she felt might be willing to help her. Becky. It was worth a try.

Dressing and tiptoeing to the kitchen, Daniella started a pot of coffee and waited. Jake came through, filled a mug and went outside to do chores. Isaac did the same, only he headed for the stand of maples, ostensibly to get a better look at the ground in the daylight.

Becky was already dressed for the office and had her darker hair pulled into a tight chignon when she appeared. "Morning. Sorry I don't have time for breakfast," she said, filling a travel mug and adding cream.

"No problem." Daniella cleared her throat. "Um, would you be planning to go anywhere near Arlington this morning?"

"Yes." The other woman's eyebrows arched and she cocked her head. "Why do you ask?"

"Well, I was just thinking…"

"Bad idea," Becky quipped, smiling and picking up her briefcase. "I heard what happened last night while I was gone."

Reaching out to stop her from leaving, Daniella willed her to understand without a great deal of explanation. "That's why I need a ride to Arlington," she said. "You know it's too dangerous for your family if I hang around here."

"Okay. So?"

"So, I'd like you to help me get away."

She raised her hands, palms out. "Whoa. Why ask me? Why don't you appeal to Isaac? He's the one with the law enforcement connections."

"Because I'm afraid he's part of the reason I'm stuck here. I think he told the marshals to take their time because he wants me to stay."

"He'd never do anything to endanger anyone. He's too conscientious for that."

"I know. But he hasn't pushed it, either, has he? After what happened last night, you and I both know the best choice for everybody is my hitting the road ASAP."

"Can't argue with you there." Becky placed her purse

and briefcase on the table and took a sip from her travel mug. "What do you propose we tell the guys? My brothers are smart enough to see right through a ruse."

"We leave a note and don't specify much. I'll just tell them I went to town with you on business. That will be true. I need to visit a safe-deposit box."

"Isaac will blow his stack!"

"Yes, but he won't have much recourse unless he guesses where I'm headed, and there's no clue to that. My father doesn't know about the bank, either. We should be perfectly safe." She began to smile as she realized Becky was no longer coming up with arguments.

"Well, don't just stand there. Go grab your purse, write the note and let's get out of here."

Starting away, Daniella skidded to a stop. "There's one more thing. Will you take good care of Puddy? He loves women. It's men and dogs he's not crazy about."

"Oh, now, wait a minute. You didn't say anything about keeping your cat."

"Please? Just for a little while? As soon as I'm settled I'll send for him."

"You can't do that unless your father's been arrested."

"We can hope that happens soon," she said with a broadening grin and a soaring spirit. "I prayed about it a lot last night."

The incredulous look on Becky's face was laughable. Daniella understood how the other woman felt. She could hardly believe the change in her own attitude, either. She was about to go against the advice of the K-9 officer and probably the marshals' office, too, yet there was an indescribable joy and lightness in her heart that defied description.

As she reached for her shoulder bag and slung the strap over her head to cross her torso, she realized that for the first time in longer than she could recall, she was truly happy.

How the idea of disregarding authority had brought that about was baffling, yet true. She felt free. Unburdened. As if she could accomplish anything if she merely put her mind to it.

Becky already had the car running when Daniella dashed out the front door and down the porch steps and slid into the passenger seat.

"Go, go, go. I think I heard Isaac coming in."

"Did you leave the note?"

"Yes." Daniella nodded rapidly.

Her heart was racing. She refused to dwell on what he might feel when he read her brief sentences. She wasn't doing this just for herself. She was doing it for him, too. And for his family. In the short time she'd known them, they had become very dear to her. Especially Isaac, she admitted silently. He was one of a kind. Someday he'd make a wonderful husband.

That conclusion was both correct and depressing. Her most ardent prayer for the brave man who had come to her rescue was that he find the happiness he deserved— with a woman worthy of his love. Someone with no heavy baggage. Someone who could accept his dangerous job without making herself sick imagining the worst every time he stepped out the door.

Someone…someone…other than her.

The stillness of the house instantly put Isaac on edge. The coffeepot was nearly empty. "Daniella?"

He paced through the kitchen and into the central hallway. "Daniella? Becky?"

No one answered except his brother. Jake came up behind him. "What's the matter. Did you lose the women?"

"Apparently." Isaac was frowning. "Is Becky's car gone already?"

"Uh-huh." Jacob was fidgeting.

"Okay. Spill it. What do you know that I don't?"

"This." Jake produced a scrap of paper and handed it over. "It was on the kitchen table."

Isaac quickly scanned it once, then slowed his mind to read it more carefully. One thing was clear. Daniella was gone. "This is a goodbye note. Do you think she really left here with Becky?"

"Probably. She couldn't see through the broken glass to drive her own car."

"Becky wouldn't help her voluntarily, would she?"

Shrugging, Jacob shoved his hands into the pockets of his well-worn jeans. "Who knows what women will do? They might have decided to band together, you know, like a sisterhood."

"I thought Becky had more sense."

"And I thought Daniella would be too scared to leave after last night. I guess we were both wrong."

Isaac's eyes widened as the full portent of the situation occurred to him. "Do you suppose they were kidnapped?"

"Naw. Becky's armed and dangerous, remember? And I've heard the lungs on your nurse friend. She can howl so loud they'd hear her in downtown DC."

Isaac fisted his phone. "All right. I'm going to call it in as a BOLO—be on the lookout. If they're just acting foolish, no harm will be done."

"And if they didn't leave of their own free will?"

Once again Isaac scanned the note in his hand. "This looks legit to me. I'll run it by the guys in the lab and see if they can tell what kind of mood she was in when she wrote it. That will tell us something."

"Not much," Jake countered.

Isaac glared at him. "You got a better idea?"

"Yeah. I say we head for the city. You deliver the note, then we keep in touch by phone and cruise DC."

"In all that traffic? What makes you think we'll be able to spot Becky's car in a mess like that?"

"Would you rather sit here and stew or be out trying to find them?"

His brother's suggestion made sense. Good thing, too, Isaac mused, since losing Daniella had already turned his thoughts into a maelstrom of confusion.

Abby was circling his feet as if she knew something was about to happen.

"All right," Isaac said. "Let's go. I'll make my call to headquarters from the car, then we'll link up by cell and keep in touch while we drive. They can't be too far ahead of us."

Checking his watch, Jacob agreed. "Want me to start with the real estate office and see if Becky showed up for work?"

"Fine. I'll check in with McCord and brief him in person, then hit the streets if they haven't been located by then. If I were a betting man, I wouldn't give our chances very good odds."

"You were the one telling her that God loved her," Jake reminded him. "Maybe it's time you told yourself the same thing."

Isaac knew his brother was right but spouting platitudes was far easier than actually living as if he had total trust in the Lord. Like all men, he was fallible.

And, like all men, his faith could falter. That didn't mean it wasn't valid. It simply pointed out that he was human. That he could care so much that his heart's desires overwhelmed common sense. He knew the chances of Daniella and Becky getting into trouble in the city were slim, yet he couldn't help worrying.

Ordering Abby into the safety compartment of the SUV instead of her crate, he ruffled her droopy ears before closing the door. Too bad he didn't have the dog's attitude about life. Every day was an adventure to her as long as her partner was along for the ride.

It occurred to Isaac that that was his biggest problem. He wanted his human partner with him, too.

Whether it was sensible or not, he wanted Daniella. It was as simple as that. And as complicated.

Becky chuckled at her companion. "Will you stop fidgeting? We're not being followed."

"How can you be sure in all this traffic?"

"Because I've been watching my mirrors ever since we left home. And, in case you haven't noticed, I've been getting on and off the beltway just for kicks."

Daniella settled back in her seat and folded her arms across her chest. "I noticed. I haven't seen anybody following us, either, but you can never be too careful."

"Is your father really that spiteful?"

"Humph. How would you feel if you'd watched your mother die the way I did?"

"Oh, I get it," Becky said. "It's just that you're his flesh-and-blood daughter. I can't imagine anybody being so callous."

"He probably wouldn't be after me if I had kept my mouth shut about Mom, but I couldn't bear the thought of him getting away with murder." She pulled a sour face. "Too bad my testimony was for nothing. He got out of prison, anyway."

"True. And unfair. What I don't understand is why you have to do this yourself. What did the witness protection people say when you told them you wanted to leave the program?"

"They advised me to wait until they were ready to officially release me." She swiveled to watch her new friend's face. "I really do believe your brother convinced them I was safer staying with him at the farm."

"I can't imagine he'd do that, although not being a guy I'm not positive. Some of them do seem to think they can handle anything and anybody." She smiled. "It's a knight-in-shining-armor complex."

Daniella's head plopped back against the raised seatback and she closed her eyes. "I can see that in Isaac. He really is a great guy."

"But?" Becky's smile grew. "I hear unspoken reservations."

Daniella nodded. "Yeah. He's not my type."

That made her companion laugh. "Sure seems like he is. The way you two look at each other tells a very different story."

"I told you. It's his job," Daniella replied. "There's nothing I hate more than explosives, and he makes a living looking for them."

"And saving lives. You admitted he's brave."

"I know I did. It's not his successes that bother me. It's the times when he makes a mistake. That could get him killed someday. I don't want to have to go through what I felt when I lost my mother."

"You had a double whammy, then," Becky said. "It was much worse because you knew your own father was responsible. Besides, Isaac and the K-9 unit are well trained. They know what they're doing."

Daniella wasn't convinced. "I don't know. I can have two similar patients in ER, give both of them the best care possible and still see one die while the other lives. Sometimes training isn't enough."

"That's because you're not God," Becky said tenderly. "It's up to you to do your job to the best of your ability, then leave the results up to Him. That's the mistake a lot of folks make. They think that they can make a difference when it's beyond human skills."

"Then why even try?" Daniella didn't necessarily disagree, to a point, but wasn't ready to relinquish a sense of control, either.

"Have you ever watched a patient recover after they were told their life was over?"

"Once in a while. Why?"

"Because I happen to believe our days are numbered, as the Bible says. I still think we can choose to squander them or cause an early demise by taking foolish chances, but something in my faith, in my heart, tells me that God has a master plan for me."

She paused, briefly glancing at her companion while she drove. "Think back. Suppose your mother had lived, you had been abused more by your father and maybe never had the courage to become a nurse or moved to DC. You wouldn't have met my family, especially Isaac, and we wouldn't be having this conversation."

"That might have been for the best," Daniella murmured.

Becky wasn't deterred. She chuckled and shook her head. "You might be able to lie to yourself enough to believe that, but you'll never convince me. We're here together, right now, because we're supposed to be."

"If that's true, are you saying that my father didn't really murder my mother?"

"Not at all. I'm saying that your mom was God's child. He knew what was going to happen and what she and her daughter needed. He released her from a life of suffering and gave you a whole new start. It was a gift, not a punishment."

"I still don't get it."

"Neither do I, most of the time," Becky admitted. "The difference is I've placed my life and my trust in God and Jesus Christ. I know He expects me to think sensibly and behave myself, but I also know He's ready for whatever happens and will always be with me."

"Does that help keep away the loneliness?"

When Becky said yes, it was so clear, so firm, Daniella had to accept it.

She retreated into her private thoughts and wondered if she'd been suffering for nothing. Had God been with her all along? Had she simply shut her eyes and her heart and mind to His presence?

There had been a time, years ago, when she'd talked to Jesus in prayer and thought she'd had enough faith to believe. What had happened to that childhood faith? Was it possible she'd been the one to distance herself because of bitterness instead of God withdrawing from her?

If that was true, what about her prayer at the top of the stairs the night before when she had simply prayed to not end up being like her father? Had she imagined the sense of calm and peace that had followed?

No. Although the feeling had been fleeting, it was as real as the car she was riding in. God *had* heard her prayer and the answer had been palpable. All she needed to do from now on was to remember that even the things she couldn't see or touch could be very real.

Without being careless, she added, leaning to peer into the outside mirror and check the traffic behind them. It was all well and good to put her trust in the wisdom of God. What she must avoid was unburdening herself too much and forgetting that she was also expected to take reasonable precautions.

If Becky was right and God had brought her to DC, that did not mean He had thrown her to the lions. Nor did it mean she couldn't leave, especially for the sake of people she cared about.

Isaac was one of those special people, she admitted, in spite of herself. In that respect she wished she'd never met him because she knew she would worry about him for the rest of her life.

And pray for his continuing safety, she added, realizing she truly believed her prayers would help. That was a breakthrough she had not seen coming and made her wonder what other surprises were lurking in the dusty corners of her heart and mind.

One thing was certain. Like it or not, Isaac Black had started to monopolize her thoughts. She could recall every moment they'd spent together as if watching the same movie, over and over.

The scariest part was that she never got to see the film all the way to the last reel and be sure everything ended well.

Unfortunately, real life was not like a romantic movie. Sometimes even the good guys didn't make it.

TWELVE

Leaving the SUV running, Isaac dashed into the lab to deliver Daniella's note to forensics, checked his own office, then trotted back out and climbed behind the wheel before he touched base with Jake. "Where are you?"

"Arlington. I swung by Becky's real estate office like I said I would. Nobody's heard from her this morning."

It took monumental effort for Isaac to control his temper. What had his sister been thinking? She knew better than to become involved with his work. Of course, this was the first time he'd taken his job home with him, so part of the blame had to be his.

"Okay," Isaac said. "If they don't know where she is, you may as well head back my way."

"Where shall we rendezvous and when?"

"How about at the Washington Monument at noon? I'd like to have another look at that site, anyway."

"Did the video copied from the TV news cameras show anything interesting?"

"No. A bunch of suits walked by me after Abby finished her sweep but we couldn't get a good look at anybody who was carrying a briefcase."

"You're sure that's what blew up?"

"Oh yeah. I saw it with my own eyes just seconds before the blast knocked me down."

"Good thing you turned away, huh?"

Isaac nodded despite the fact he was alone in the car with his dog. "Yeah." He changed the subject. "While you're at it, keep your eyes peeled for Fagan, too. He probably isn't involved this time but you might spot him."

"Not likely, bro."

"No, but our chances of being the ones who locate Becky and Daniella aren't good, either."

"It still beats pacing the floor at the house."

Isaac had to agree. The only drawback so far had been finding a direct order on his desk giving him an additional assignment.

"Listen, Jake, my captain was called away and left me instructions to go interview Congressman Jeffries ASAP. I'm going to run by the Capitol and see if I can catch Jeffries in his office before you and I link up again. It shouldn't take long. I'll leave my phone on vibrate in case you need to reach me. The local police are covering the city, so why don't you go back by Becky's office and keep an eye out there for a while?"

"That probably makes more sense than driving all over town for nothing, especially since she's not answering her cell. I just hate to feel so useless."

"I know what you mean," Isaac told him. "But now that I'm past the initial shock of the note, I think it's the smartest thing we can do."

Jake huffed cynically. "Having Becky wandering around out here is bad enough. Daniella with her makes it a hundred times worse."

"No argument there. If—when—we locate them I'll let you scold our sister while I read Daniella the riot act."

"Sometimes you sound just like Grandpa Black."

"I know." He chuckled. "From what I can remember

about him, I'll take that as a compliment. He was quite a character."

"Stubborn as a mule, as Grandma used to say. Listen, baby brother, be careful out there."

"I will. Bye."

Isaac meant it. He was always careful, always on guard, unless he was relaxing at home. And now even the farm wasn't safe.

"Whose fault was that?" he muttered to himself.

His, of course. He had been the one to insist Daniella stay with him and had also contacted the marshals' office. How was he to know Fagan had hidden a bug in her apartment and listened to the whole conversation? The only good thing about that man's confession was learning that he hadn't been savvy enough to capture their cell signals as first assumed.

That gave Isaac a small measure of peace. A detailed knowledge of electronics would make Fagan's already dangerous bag of tricks far, far deadlier.

Until she actually saw the banded stacks of bills in the safe-deposit box, Daniella wasn't sure they'd still be there. Her hands were shaking as she shoved them into the canvas tote she'd borrowed from Becky and zipped the top closed.

The door to that section of the vault stood open. "I'm finished," she said as she passed the young bank employee who had assisted her.

"Was everything all right?" the woman asked pleasantly.

"Just fine." Daniella knew better than to give any indication of unrest. Considering the acting she'd had to do these past few days, not to mention during the preceding ten years, she figured she should be nominated for a professional performance award, red carpet and all.

The bank seemed unduly crowded as she emerged from the quietude of the vault area. It was hard to keep from scanning the bank's customers so rapidly that she gave the impression of nervousness. In truth, she was growing frantic now that she had her nest egg in hand. It wasn't the money itself that gave her qualms, it was what it could bring to her life, her future. If she left DC on her own, even if she later returned as she hoped to, she'd need cash to set herself up the way the witness protection program had before.

Although she saw no evident threat, her skin tingled and her heart raced. Instinct told her to get out of there as soon as she could, rejoin Becky and hit the road.

Weaving between bank customers and employees, she hugged the tote and her purse close and headed for the heavy glass doors. An elderly security guard near the front exit smiled at her and touched the brim of his cap.

Daniella hardly noticed. By this time the sense of impending doom had burgeoned into a full-blown panic attack. She assumed she'd feel better once she was back outside on the street, but that didn't happen.

On the contrary, emerging into the sunlight and seeing all the foot and vehicle traffic made her feel as if she were being suffocated.

There had been no available parking spots when they'd arrived, so Becky had let her out at the curb and promised to keep circling the block. Where was she?

Scanning passing cars, she forced herself to stand still when what she yearned to do was run. Fast and far. Away from the familiar city and into the oblivion of some place where she wasn't known.

The hair on the back of her neck prickled. She started to turn to go back into the bank to wait for Becky.

No. Don't do that, she countered, not comprehending why she was so sure, yet willing to follow the strongest impulse of the many pulling her right and left like a rag doll about to be ripped apart by warring children.

She hesitated. Almost stumbled. Swiveled back to scan the street once more.

A familiar compact car double-parked right in front of her. "Come on!"

Daniella was off the curb and jumping into Becky's passenger seat in mere seconds. She dropped the tote on the floor beneath her feet.

Whipping back into traffic, Becky dodged the slower-moving cars and made an illegal left turn at the next corner.

Daniella was struggling to fasten her seat belt. "I can't buckle up if you don't stop throwing me around." As she finished speaking, she glanced at her friend. "What's the matter?"

"I don't know. Maybe it was the look on your face when I picked you up or maybe it was something I saw in the background, but all I could think about was getting away."

"Me, too!" Wide-eyed, Daniella looked back over her shoulder. The impression that one of the men in the crowd might be Terence Fagan was intense.

Realizing that her mind could be playing tricks on her, she straightened and forced a smile. "Sorry my jumpiness has rubbed off on you. There's no way my father could have known about my safe-deposit box ahead of time."

"You're probably right," Becky said, "but it's possible that he either had us followed or did it himself, even with all my evasive tactics."

"I'm sure he was the prowler who shot out the window in my car, too." She noted her friend's arching eyebrows.

"After he showed up in the marshal's car and tried to drag you off, do you have any *doubt*?"

"I suppose not." Daniella blew a noisy sigh, then leaned down, pulled one bundle out of the tote and separated the bills. Some she stuffed into her purse, the rest she tried to hand to Becky.

"What's that for?"

"Damages and whatever else you need to stay safe after I'm gone."

"I've been giving that some thought," Becky said. "I wonder if hitting the road on your own is the smartest move."

"Of course it is. It's the only way to be sure my father doesn't continue to harass you."

"What if he doesn't know you've left?"

Growing pensive, Daniella pressed her lips into a thin line. "I'll drive my car. That will tell him."

"Not until we get the windshield replaced," Becky countered. "You have to be able to see where you're going."

"Very funny." Now that they were blocks from the bank and beginning to move faster, Daniella was able to manage a real smile. "I could always hang out the side window or look around those big, radiating cracks."

"Right."

"Or buy a new car. I have enough money to pay cash. Want to take me to a dealership?"

"That won't solve the problem. If you buy a car off a lot there will still be a paper trail. I think your best option is getting something else from an individual and holding off on the transfer of title."

"Okay. I've never had a car window repaired. How is it done?"

"On scene mostly," Becky said. "I'll stop by my office and place the order."

"Not if it's going to take long," Daniella warned. "I plan to be out of here before tonight."

"I think the glass guy will squeeze you in if I tell him it's an emergency."

"Offer to double his fee," Daniella told her. "Whatever it takes to get it done right away."

"You mean before Isaac figures out you're back at the house, don't you?"

Nodding forcefully, Daniella said, "Oh yeah. Way before that."

The trip to visit Congressman Jeffries's Capitol Hill office building was easy. Isaac parked the SUV in a shady spot reserved for law enforcement, reported his location to headquarters and left the windows rolled partway down to keep Abby cool.

His badge got him past the guards at the entrance without delay. Knowing where Jeffries's private office was saved time, too. Isaac turned right at the second hallway and followed it to nicer quarters than many congressmen managed to get. Space was worth more than gold in DC, and having enough room to turn around, let alone comfortably employ a small staff, was a real boon.

Rather than phone ahead, Isaac had taken the chance he'd catch Jeffries there. Judging by the startled expression on his secretary's face as she took in his full image—uniform, badge, K-9 patches and cap with an identical logo—he had made the right decision.

She blushed, then smiled tentatively. "I'm sorry, officer, the congressman is in conference."

"I can wait." He removed his cap, folded it and looped it through his belt.

"I don't advise waiting. Congressman Jeffries has appointments all day and a state dinner to attend this evening."

"Who is he meeting with right now?"

She hesitated, so instead of giving her time to warn her boss, Isaac strode across the carpeted floor to the heavy mahogany door, knocked once and tried the knob. It turned freely.

The loyal secretary attempted to block his way and failed. "I'm sorry, sir. I told him you were busy."

Two men in luxuriously tailored suits stood with iced amber-colored drinks in hand. The taller, gray-haired one was Harland Jeffries. Isaac recognized the other as Leon Ridge, one of the congressman's longtime aides. Neither appeared overjoyed to see him.

Professional politician to the nth degree, Jeffries left his aide and approached Isaac, offering a hand of welcome. "Good to see you. Leon and I were just finishing up. I can give you a couple of minutes, if that will suffice."

"That should be fine. Captain McCord would have come himself but he was called out of town unexpectedly, so he asked me to fill in for him."

"Fine, fine. Gavin's a good man. Very loyal. We go way back, you know."

"Yes, I know." Isaac stared pointedly at Leon Ridge. "Do you mind?"

Jeffries answered for him. "No problem. Leon was just leaving." He used a glance to direct the younger man to the rear door. "You know what I need done. We're finished for now."

There was something about Ridge that made Isaac's

skin crawl. Always had, although he had no concrete reason to feel that way other than the fact that Abby and the other Capitol K-9 Unit dogs wouldn't allow the man to get near them. That judgment was good enough for Isaac.

"Just a few simple questions if you don't mind, sir," Isaac said to Harland Jeffries.

He took the chair Jeffries indicated and watched him settle in on the opposite side of the ornate desk, straighten a few file folders, then lean back and lace his fingers behind his head. The studied pose would have looked more casual if he had bothered to remove his jacket or loosen his tie.

"So, what can I do for you? I hope you've come to tell me that the woman who killed my poor Michael is finally in custody."

"What woman?" Isaac asked, purposely toying with him.

"Erin Eagleton. The one who must have shot him and me. Don't you people talk to each other?"

There was no proof that Erin Eagleton, who'd been Michael Jeffries's girlfriend, shot anyone. Though a charm from her necklace had been found at the murder scene, Jeffries had said several times that he didn't know who had murdered his son and then had turned the gun on him, leaving him for dead. "She's still missing as far as I know. But that's not why I'm here."

Jeffries lowered his arms, rested his elbows on the desk and steepled his fingers. "Oh?"

"You see, sir, it's like this. We're not getting very far in our investigation into the attack during your press conference and we were wondering if you'd had any more thoughts about who may have placed the explosive device."

"Since you haven't found Erin Eagleton yet, what about her?"

"Why would she want to harm you?" Isaac took note of a slight tic at the corner of the congressman's eye, indicating nervousness he wasn't managing to mask completely.

"Maybe she thinks I can identify her. I don't know. It's your responsibility to find out these things, not mine. Do your job." Jeffries got to his feet. "This interview is over."

Isaac nodded and offered his hand, satisfied that he'd made a little progress.

Leaving the building, Isaac was more than happy to get back to looking for Daniella and Becky. Because of Daniella's cryptic farewell note, he wasn't too worried about foul play, but that didn't mean the women hadn't accidentally gotten themselves into trouble. Daniella seemed to have a talent for it, and his sister wasn't much better. Anybody who enjoyed landing jets on a pitching carrier deck in the middle of the ocean the way Becky used to had to be too brave for her own good.

As soon as he was outside on the walkway, he pulled out his cell and speed-dialed Jacob.

"Any sign of them?"

"Yeah. I just missed catching them at Becky's office. One of the brokers said she and another woman stopped by for info on a repairman, then split."

"Did they say where they were going?"

"No," Jake told him, "but I have a good idea I know, anyway."

"Well, spit it out before I go crazy. Where?"

"They called a glass man to have a car windshield and side windows replaced. Where do you think they're headed?"

Isaac let out a whoop. "The farm!"

"That's kinda what I figured. You want me to go see?"

"I'll meet you there. When you pull in, try to block her car with yours in case she decides to make a run for it. I'll do the same."

"You really mean you're not going to let her go if that's what she wants?"

Isaac heard sadness in his voice when he said, "Oh, I'll let her go. I just want to be sure we don't read about her murder in the newspaper. I'll do whatever I have to in order to keep her safe and sound."

"She is going to be madder than a wet hen."

Isaac was so relieved to have learned where to look for the women, it was easy to laugh at his brother's comment. "Now who sounds like Grandpa Black?" he asked with a chuckle. "Just see that you're there, too. I may need backup."

Jake laughed, too. "Bro, if you decide to tangle with those two stubborn women, you're going to need more than me for backup. You're going to need the Virginia National Guard!"

THIRTEEN

Daniella was both elated and depressed, causing untold problems with her psyche. She desperately wanted to run from the danger her father posed, yet the moment she laid eyes on the Blacks' farmhouse she was filled with a sense of home. Friends. Even family.

Wheeling into the familiar driveway, Becky checked her out, frowned and asked, "You okay?"

"Yes. I'm just conflicted. I know it's best that I disappear but I really hate to leave this place."

"Leave Isaac, you mean?"

"Him, too, of course." Knowing that her cheeks had to be aflame, she averted her face and stared out the car windows as if she found the passing fence unduly fascinating.

Becky chuckled softly. "Of course."

"Hey, this is no laughing matter," Daniella insisted, turning back. "I never dreamed I'd someday meet a man who appealed to me the way your brother does, and then when I do, he has the worst job in the world."

"What makes you think you couldn't get used to it if you loved him enough?"

"That's another thing. The more I care about him, the more scared I get that I'll lose him the same way I lost my mother."

"Like I said, you need to trust God more."

"Why? So I'll have divine comfort when Isaac is blown to bits? No thanks."

"All I can do is tell you what's helped me. The more I tried to figure out my life, the more confused I got. But when I turned it over to the Lord and stopped insisting that everything go the way I'd planned, the results were far better than I'd imagined."

"Let go, you mean?"

"In a manner of speaking. I see it more as rolling with the punches. It's not so much what happens to us as it is how we react to adversity."

Daniella was arguing within, and some of that attitude spilled out into the conversation. "Look. I was only seventeen when I went into witness protection. I've already made up my mind I'm going to run now but eventually return. I have a career that I happen to love and won't abandon. I'm just not going to make the mistake I did the other night in my poor car. I plan to duck, literally and figuratively, then counterattack later, if I have to."

"How do you propose to do that? This is not the Old West and you're no gunfighter."

Agreeing, Daniella nodded slowly, thoughtfully. "I know. I keep thinking there must be some way I can win. I just haven't found it yet."

Becky drove to the rear of the old Victorian and parked, then swiveled to look directly at her passenger. "When I took you to the bank this morning I was positive that helping you hit the road was for the best. Now I'm not so sure."

"Why not?"

"Because it has occurred to me that God may have placed you with us for a reason. Think about it. You're not trained for combat but the three of us are, to varying degrees, and if you stick around it will be like having three bodyguards with at least one of us on duty at all times."

"You're not part of this. You shouldn't have to risk your lives just because my father is out to get me."

"If that's all there was to it you'd be right. But suppose we were put into your life for a purpose? What if we'd be wrong to let you go?"

"Suppose you let me decide about that."

Becky spread her hands, palms up. "Okay. Fair enough. As long as you keep an open mind. I think, while your car is being repaired, you should give the marshals another call. It's quite possible they may be preparing to whisk you away or something."

"I sincerely doubt that. I told them I wanted out of their program. Period."

"You'll never know what's going on if you don't ask. Suppose my brother did pull strings to get them to leave you in limbo?"

Daniella brightened. "Do you really think so?" She stepped out of the car when Becky did, greeted the excited farm dogs with pats on their heads, then led the way toward the back porch.

There was something so special about this farm, this house, she was in awe. There were no adequate words to describe how she felt about the Black family, particularly Isaac, and no amount of internal arguing against those feelings fazed her conclusions.

Sticking close, the largest of the mixed-breed dogs bumped her leg and began to growl. The rumble in his throat was enough to bring Daniella up short. She spread her arms like a human gate. "Becky?"

"What's wrong?"

"This dog is growling."

Becky joined her and bent over the enormous canine

to listen. "He *is*. In all the years we've had him, this is the first time I've heard him act mean. Did you do something different?"

"Not me." She eyed the wooden porch. "Shut the dogs in the barn and stay back. I want to take a closer look and I don't want any company."

The notion that a dog that had never been trained for defense was trying to tell her something struck Daniella as improbable. Nevertheless, she had always had an affinity for animals and could read their body language well. This dog was definitely put off by something. It was conceivable that he'd become sensitized to some sights or odors by watching Abby work.

Cautious, purposeful steps brought her around to the open end of the porch. She bent down. Peered into the dimness below the wooden deck.

At first, all she saw were spiderwebs and dust. Then, squinting, she managed to isolate a dark shape that didn't look as if it belonged there.

Daniella gasped, straightened and gaped at Becky. Before she could sound the warning, the rear door opened and Jake stepped out. "About time you decided to show up," he said. "Isaac and I've been all over the city looking for you two."

Becky raised her arms as if sheer willpower could stop her brother's progress.

Beside the porch, Daniella was close enough to grab the hem of his jeans and shout, "Don't move!"

One thing Isaac had not expected was a call from his sister. The moment he recognized her voice he started to scold. "Do you know what you've done? Jake and I looked everywhere. I can't believe you'd agree to take Daniella into the city, let alone not keep in touch. You…"

Jumbling with the sound of his own voice was the rapid-fire speech of his sister. It was her evident agitation that caused him to hesitate. "What?"

"I said, there's a bomb under the porch and Jake is standing on it. Where are you?"

"Five minutes out. Nobody move. Understand? The slightest jiggle could set it off."

Becky, usually the most levelheaded of all the women Isaac knew, sounded near hysteria. "Didn't you check before you left?" she screeched.

"I was in kind of a hurry, thanks to you. Abby and I went out the back and she didn't alert."

"Well, she would now."

"Somebody must have placed a device when all of us were away. I'm pulling off the highway. Sit tight."

With both hands fisted on the wheel and his siren wailing, Isaac floored the gas pedal. These two-lane country roads weren't designed for high-speed driving, but as long as he stuck to the center line he should be able to negotiate the corners without sliding off into a ditch.

Living in the country rather than the city had made him too complacent. He should have taken more pains to protect his family. It was his fault for bringing trouble home with him, but what else could he have done?

"I could have turned her over to the authorities as soon as Abby detected that first bomb," he murmured. His fist hammered the steering wheel. Why hadn't he? And why, given her father's early release, had he continued to encourage her stay with them? It might not be the dumbest stunt he'd ever pulled, but it was close.

Wheeling into the long drive leading to the farmhouse, Isaac slowed to keep from losing control of the car on the loose dirt and gravel. He parked on the grass before getting too close and jumped out, half running, half limping toward the place Becky had cited.

When he rounded the corner of the house and saw the entire picture, his heart leaped into his throat, pounding wildly.

Jake was just outside the back door all right, and Becky was nearest the barn. It was Daniella's position that tied his gut in knots and floored him. She was standing beside the raised wooden deck with one hand on the closest support and the other clutching Jake's jeans at the ankle.

Even if the bomb detonated and the others were blown clear, there was no chance of Daniella escaping in one piece. None at all.

Thankful that he'd left Abby in the SUV, Isaac boldly approached. Becky spotted him first and screeched his name.

Jake's head swiveled slowly and he quirked a smile.

Daniella was the only one who didn't move, so he called out to her as he drew closer. "If you're not putting any weight on the porch, you can let go of him."

She shook her head, her hair swinging.

Close enough to touch her, he laid a hand lightly on her shoulder and spoke softly so he wouldn't frighten her more. "Let him go, Daniella. Open your hand."

"No. This is all my fault. I'll stay as long as Jake has to."

"I notified my office as soon as I got Becky's call," Isaac said, "but they won't send the bomb squad until I report what I've found."

He edged to one side and shined a flashlight into the recesses beneath the porch. "Where did you see it?"

"Under a step. There's a blinking light."

"I don't see what you're describing. Are you sure?"

"Yes. No. I don't know."

Isaac backed out and straightened. "All right. Since you say what you saw was under a step and there's absolutely nothing attached to the porch, Jake can go back inside."

"Really?"

"Yes. Really." He looked to his brother. "Just take it easy and don't slam the door."

Isaac wrapped his arms around Daniella and drew her in the opposite direction, holding his breath until they were in the clear. Then he turned her and pulled her closer, relieved to feel her arms slip around him, as well. Judging by the severity of her trembling, she was good and scared. And foolishly brave.

"Easy. I've got you," he whispered against her silky hair. "What in the world did you think you'd accomplish by getting yourself blown up?"

"I couldn't leave him. I just couldn't." Her arms tightened around Isaac's waist and she laid her cheek on his chest.

The notion that she was ready to sacrifice herself for his brother was both comforting and disturbing. If she cared that much for Jake, perhaps he was the one who was destined to win her heart. Isaac wondered if he would be able to stay close to his family if that did happen. He doubted it. Picturing Daniella as anyone's wife but his was already tearing him apart. To actually see it happen would be sheer agony.

The click of the latch on the front door echoed in the rural stillness. Becky had already joined Isaac and Daniella by the K-9 patrol unit when Jake jogged up and put his strong arms around the group.

Isaac tolerated the closeness for a few long seconds before setting Daniella away and issuing orders. "All of you climb in and wait out here. I'm going to start by working Abby around the house."

Daniella reached out to him, grasped his forearm. "Do you have to go?"

"It's my job. I told you. I need to have the entire area screened and report before they'll start the bomb squad. They may not need to."

Becky had already slid into the second seat. Daniella reluctantly joined her while Jake stood outside. He inclined his head and motioned with his eyes. "Quite a woman."

"Yes." *And I saw her first*, Isaac wanted to add. Instead, he circled the unit. Abby was ready to go, as always. He fitted and fastened her vest, then snapped on a long lead.

One glance back was all he allowed himself before he and his canine partner went to work.

Watching from the car, Daniella was alternately wringing her hands and clamping her fingers together so tightly they whitened.

She squeezed her eyes closed and didn't realize she'd been praying until she heard herself saying, "Please, please keep him safe."

Becky added, "Amen," and joined their folded hands. "Father, thank You for keeping the rest of us safe today, too, and bless my brother as he does his job."

As soon as Daniella looked up, Becky smiled. "I think it's important to thank Him for the good things, too. Otherwise we sound like spoiled children, always begging for cookies for dessert without being grateful for the whole meal we had before."

"I—I never thought of it that way." She kept hold of

her friend's hand. "I guess I should spend more time giving thanks for not being in the car with my mom."

"And for meeting Isaac in the ER," Becky added. "Looking back, I can easily imagine a divine purpose. You needed special friends and allies, and He sent you to us."

"That is a comforting thought," she replied. "I just hope everybody survives our adventure together."

"Even your dad?" Becky asked gently.

Astounded, Daniella didn't know how to answer. What was wrong with her? For years she'd nurtured her abhorrence of that man, so where was the fire in her heart and mind now? Terence Fagan was still causing her trouble and had undoubtedly placed the first bomb under her car, so why couldn't she easily agree that she wished him dead?

Daniella looked over with unshed tears blurring her vision and said, "I don't know anymore."

Becky gave her hands a squeeze. "Good for you."

"But he's just as evil as he always was. What's wrong with me?"

Smiling, Becky too looked misty-eyed. "It's not what's wrong with you, honey. It's more about what's getting right."

"You mean with God?"

"Among other things. Holding on to bitterness can kill a person almost as easily as a bullet. You should know. I'm sure you've had patients who left this earth cursing their fate and the other people they blamed for it."

"A few. It always struck me as a shame that they held on to grudges with their last thoughts. Such a waste."

"Amen, sister," Becky said, dashing away sparse tears and breaking into a smile. "You're really a quick learner."

"Ha! Tell that to your brother. He thinks I'm an idiot."

"No, he doesn't. And I assume you mean Isaac."

Blushing again, Daniella stared at her clasped hands as if they were the most interesting things she'd ever seen. "Yes. Isaac."

"We all have baggage," Becky said.

Daniella met her gaze. "Not everybody's baggage is lethal the way mine is."

FOURTEEN

Isaac was so relieved when Abby didn't alert to whatever was tucked under the back porch he almost laughed out loud. Cursory examination identified the object as an old metal lunch pail that he concluded had probably been left there when the house was far newer. As for the flashing light Daniella had claimed to have seen, he could only imagine sunlight glinting off something nearby.

Following standard procedure, mostly out of habit, he continued the sweep of the yard and shrubbery, so positive that he'd come up empty he smiled at his K-9 partner.

Tail held erect in the position that was called flagging, Abby went gaily about her task, poking her sensitive nose into flower beds and tufts of grass as if playing a fascinating game.

That's what this is to her, Isaac reminded himself. Hers was one of the only jobs he could think of where lack of success was the desired result. He'd much rather reward her for *not* finding a bomb than deal with other possibilities.

Isaac's smile grew. "What's the matter, girl? Do you wish you were out chasing rabbits?"

Snuffling, she kept her nose buried in the grass next to one of the outdoor entrances that led directly into the basement. That small door closed off a coal chute, a left-over necessity from the days when the old house was heated by a coal-fired furnace.

Isaac frowned. Paused. Gave her more lead and watched closely. He sensed her decision a few seconds before she plopped down into a sitting position and began to quiver all over.

Transfixed, Isaac tapped his ear to activate the radio transmitter in his earpiece. "Capitol K-9 Unit Five," he reported. "Dog has alerted. Send the bomb squad stat." He recited his address, then added, "It's my place. Abby just told me there's a bomb under my house."

Daniella elbowed Becky with a sharp, "Look." Jacob had stopped leaning against the SUV and was clearly on his way to join Isaac. "What do you think?"

"Both of them usually have more casual body language," Becky offered. "If I had to guess, I'd say Abby found something."

"That's what I thought." Daniella hugged herself. "I hope we're both wrong."

"Only one way to find out."

"I thought you'd never get around to saying so. Let's go ask."

They clambered out and joined ranks, shoulder to shoulder, to approach the brothers. Daniella began, "I was right, wasn't I?" It shocked and puzzled her when Isaac shook his head.

"Well, if you didn't find anything, then why do you look as if you're mad at the world?" She made a face. "Or is it me?"

"I'm not mad at you," Isaac assured her. "Not for convincing me to search for explosives, at any rate. I'm still pretty steamed at the goodbye note and disappearing act, though."

"Never mind all that. What did Abby find?"

"I'm not positive. We won't be until the bomb disposal squad arrives. But she did alert. It just didn't happen to be in the place that scared you."

"What?" Daniella's head snapped around and she scowled at each of the others in turn, beginning and ending with Isaac. "There was something under the porch. I saw it myself. It was rectangular and about this long." She held her hands parallel to demonstrate.

"That was nothing but an old rusty lunch box, probably an antique from the looks of it. It was the other side of the house Abby told me was dangerous."

"Oh, my…" She swayed as the truth hit home and felt Becky grab her arm. "I have never been happier to be proved wrong, even if I do feel foolish."

Slowly shaking his head, Isaac told her, "You may want to rethink that. If you hadn't spotted what you thought was a bomb and called me, we might all have lost our lives."

"A blessing in disguise?" his sister asked.

"Yes. And not that well disguised if all the perp did was slide it down the old coal chute into the basement. We're fortunate it didn't accidentally detonate when it hit bottom."

The full significance of his words sank in slowly, making Daniella wish she didn't understand quite so well. Once again she had brought her personal troubles to others and once again they had narrowly escaped.

It took her several minutes to calm herself enough to speak her mind. She reached out to Isaac. Touched his arm for a brief moment. "I was going to just hit the road, for your sake, but since it's gone this far, maybe I should recontact the marshals' office like Becky suggested and see what they say."

"You actually *want* to leave."

"I have to. Don't you get it? As long as I'm here, Fagan will keep trying to hurt me and you'll all be in his cross-hairs."

"Okay. Two things," Isaac said, looking deeply into her eyes and making her feel like a butterfly specimen displayed in a collector's box.

"Go ahead. But I'm right and you know it."

He massaged the back of his neck with one hand while continuing to make direct eye contact. "First, there's no way for Fagan to know you've moved away from us unless we post a big sign on the lawn and he believes it. Second, we need to figure out how he knew we were all going to be gone at the same time so he could plant this new bomb."

"He couldn't have known. I only thought of my traveling money and asked Becky for a ride to Arlington this morning." She paused, eyes widening. "Could he have lied about leaving a bug in my apartment just to make us feel complacent about other options?"

"That had occurred to me," Isaac said flatly.

"Uh-oh."

Isaac agreed. "You can say that again. If he has different means of eavesdropping we'll have to be a lot more careful about what we say. I'll put the Capitol K-9 Unit's tech wizard, Fiona, to work on the problem as soon as we're cleared to reenter the house. She can check cell phones and our computers to make sure he hasn't tapped into those systems."

"I could just hit the road and check in once in a while," Daniella offered.

"How? From where? With what, a compromised cell phone?"

"Email, maybe? I could stop at coffee shops or libraries and use their computers."

"Only if you're sure your father didn't learn any new tricks in prison. It was your idea that he might have taught other inmates his skills. Suppose they shared theirs with him? If he's half as smart as you are, I wouldn't put it past him."

"Thanks—I think."

"You're welcome. There's also the possibility he contacted another relocated witness who managed to get him the information he needed."

"Now you're really reaching."

"I know. But we can't overlook any possibilities, no matter how remote."

"Look. It's not that complicated," Daniella insisted. "My father saw me on the TV news."

"And reached your apartment while you were still at work, set a bomb and got away clean? I strongly doubt that was all the time he had."

"You think he was already closing in?"

Isaac soberly agreed. "He had to be. The newscast may have helped with the final details, but it's hard to believe he could have come to DC and accomplished all he did, like planting that bug in your apartment or the bomb on your car, if he hadn't had some prior knowledge."

"I—I don't know what to say." Daniella was speaking softly, hesitantly. How could she argue with a professional? Besides, wasn't one branch of law enforcement supposed to have an in with the others? If that were the case, how could she be certain that somebody in *Washington* hadn't tipped off her father?

So, who else would care about her true identity, let

alone suspect she was in hiding? Was she sending signals that told people she was a fugitive from injustice and homicide? Could she possibly be that transparent?

A blurred picture began to emerge. How difficult would it be for a man with underworld connections like Terence Fagan to find the weakest link in a chain and either bribe or threaten enough to coerce someone into giving him access to her personal files?

Considering what she knew about her father and what she'd witnessed growing up, she was surprised he hadn't knocked on her door and exacted his revenge months ago.

Her gaze locked with Isaac's. "Are you positive you want me to stick around? I mean seriously. Think about it. You'll be risking your homestead and folks you care about. That makes no sense to me."

"Maybe that's because you've never belonged to a close family. We stand up for each other and for our special friends. They'd do the same for me."

"Am I a special friend? Is that what you're saying?" Daniella managed to ask the question without showing too much emotion, but by the time he got around to answering she was starting to feel the welling of unshed tears.

Stepping closer, he said, "If I have my way, you'll be an official member of my family someday. In the meantime, consider yourself adopted."

She didn't answer. Couldn't speak, let alone reply with any degree of confidence. Was he intimating that he had serious feelings for her? That was awful. And wonderful. And everything in between.

Isaac closed her gaping mouth with one finger under her chin, then leaned and kissed her gently.

Maybe it was the thought that they had just cheated death that made her so willing to accept his show of affection. At that moment, that precious moment, Daniella didn't know or care. She merely kissed him back and let herself enjoy the closeness, the rare sense of total approval.

He knew her background, her family troubles, and yet he was inviting her into his private circle. That, alone, was such a beautiful gesture she could hardly take it in.

For those brief moments when Isaac's lips caressed hers, she was the person she had always dreamed of being. And she was no longer alone.

Isaac had stayed outside with the others while the bomb squad had entered his cellar, located the device and defused it. To nobody's surprise, it matched the design of the ones Fagan was known to favor. If the fingerprints were his it would be a slam dunk.

He didn't want to break bad news to Daniella but saw no alternative. Unfortunately, their already tenuous relationship had grown even more strained since he'd given in to his heart's desire and kissed her. At the time he'd done it he'd known it was a fool's move, yet the chance she might favor his brother over him had forced him to act or perhaps pay for his inaction for the rest of his life.

Once he'd kissed her, however, he'd realized that his tender feelings were reciprocated, making him glad he'd made the move, yet sorry he'd pushed things ahead so rapidly. Under less stressful conditions, she might not have responded quite so eagerly. Then again, maybe their trying circumstances were meant to help them develop a deeper relationship more quickly than normal.

It was later in the evening, after they'd eaten supper, when Isaac heard from his boss. As he'd expected, his frank report on Jeffries's cynical attitude and nervousness during their interview had not been well accepted.

"What were you trying to do," Gavin McCord demanded, "give the man a heart attack?"

"I just asked him if he knew anything else about the bomb at his press conference. I was under the impression you sent me to question him because I have no personal ties. And speaking of bombs, I should tell you there was another explosive device planted at my farm today. The preliminary details will be coming from the bomb squad after they process the evidence." Isaac heard papers rustling in the background.

"I just got that report. Hold on."

More rustling sounds were followed by an exclamation. "Whoa. That's not what I'd expected."

"What? What did they find?"

"Fingerprints on the inside of the casing. The outside had been wiped clean but there were several good partials on the works, not that the assembly was very sophisticated. Basically just a few wires, a detonator and old-fashioned gunpowder."

"Humph. That sounds like Fagan's work."

"I'd have to agree with you if the prints were his. They're not."

"Were they able to ID the maker?"

"This says so, but there must be a mistake."

"Who was it?" Isaac wished he was face-to-face with his captain so he could judge his facial expressions.

"Not over the phone. I'd rather look into the identity question myself. I'll get back to you."

"Wait!"

McCord had ended the call. Deep in thought, Isaac decided he owed it to Daniella to inform her that her father had apparently not set this particular device. Yes, it was still possible that he'd had someone else do the construction for him and had then wiped the exterior of the box clean, but the chances of that were slim. Fagan would have wanted her to know where the bomb came from in order to increase her angst.

Isaac climbed the stairs and knocked on her closed door. "Daniella? It's me."

When an answer didn't come promptly, he knocked again, warned, "You'd better be decent because I'm coming in," and opened the door, half expecting to find her gone and the room empty.

Instead, he saw Daniella sitting on her bed, legs crossed, amid bundles of cash. Her enormous black cat was curled up atop part of the pile of bills.

Eyes wide and lips parted in surprise, she stared at him.

"What in the...?"

"This is the traveling money I mentioned. Becky took me to get it."

His heart hardened despite his tender feelings for her. "Is *that* what your father is really after?"

"Of course not. He'd have no way of knowing I'd stashed it away instead of spending it"

He saw her face change as he demanded, "Where did it come from?"

"I could tell you but I don't think I will. If you don't trust me, there's no point, is there?"

Their raised voices sent Puddy under the bed seeking sanctuary.

"I never said I didn't trust you," Isaac insisted.

"You didn't have to. I can see it in your eyes. You think I was involved in something criminal like my dad, don't you? Is that why you're spying on me?"

"I'm not spying," he said, trying to salvage the conversation before their friendship was further undermined. "I came up here to bring you good news."

Although she didn't speak, he could tell she was interested enough to let him explain.

"It's about the bomb Abby found in the basement. The prints on it weren't your father's. This time, we can't tie the bomb to him."

She unfolded her legs and slid to the edge of the bed, where she sat very still, apparently absorbing what she'd just learned.

Finally, she met his gaze. "That doesn't make any sense."

"I know." Shoving his hands into the hip pockets of his jeans, he struck a casual pose, hoping to encourage her to do the same by example.

"Whose prints were they?"

"That's another strange thing. My boss got the report of a match but he wouldn't tell me."

"Could he be the one who gave away the time of my first appointment with the marshal?"

Isaac was adamant. "No way. I've never met a more honest man. Gavin's just being cautious, that's all. He acted like he might be acquainted with the suspect and said he wanted to do more investigating before he made the lab's findings public."

Sighing, Daniella nodded. "I suppose he knows thousands of people in DC, including the White House staff."

"We all do. Our Capitol K-9 Unit is under the command of General Margaret Meyer. She has an office there as well as at unit headquarters."

"All right." She eyed the jumble of money. "You don't happen to have a big safe here, do you? I'd hate to lose the only thing my mother left me."

"That's where all that cash came from?"

Her "Yes" was faint as she raised her eyes to search the depths of his.

"I'm so sorry, honey. I assumed you were struggling to make ends meet because of where you lived and the older car you drove, and when I saw all that cash... I shouldn't have jumped to conclusions." He took a step closer, hoping she wouldn't throw him out.

"Another hazard of your job?" Daniella asked.

"Apparently. I meet a lot of criminals when I'm working. I guess it's made me cynical."

Rising, she slowly approached until she was close enough to slip her arms around his waist and step into his waiting embrace.

"Well, get over it, Mister," she said, laying her cheek against his chest. "The bomb-chasing problem is bad enough without adding a distrustful nature on top of all that constant danger."

"It's what I do," he said, kissing the top of her head and inhaling the floral sweetness of her shampoo. "I'm sorry, but it's my calling."

"The same as mine is to do all I can to nurse folks back to health. I know."

As her hug tightened and he felt her begin to tremble, Isaac realized how truly frightened his job made her. Part of that fear was understandable because of her traumatic past, but that wasn't all there was to it. He knew her well enough now to see that she was also selling herself short. There was a good chance that, even though she was attracted to him, she'd eventually pull away for good, thinking she was doing him a favor.

He knew he couldn't make her fall in love with him. However, he didn't intend to sit back idly while she forced herself to leave for all the wrong reasons. If, in the end, she wanted to disappear again, he'd support that decision. He might not like it, but he would not stand in her way.

As Isaac saw it, his most important task besides protecting her was to convince her that she could trust her own instincts. Rely on herself. Believe she deserved the happiness that had eluded her for the past ten years.

Nothing in Terence Fagan's thick file indicated that he had the slightest affection for his only child, so no one could count on him seeing the light, so to speak. What Isaac did hope was that Daniella would be able to stop identifying so strongly with her father's sins and begin to focus on the love her mother had imparted while she was alive.

Having grown up in a close family with loving parents, Isaac had trouble imagining any father developing lethal enmity for his offspring, not to mention going so far as to actually murder them.

That was one reason why so many in law enforcement doubted that Harland Jeffries could have shot his only son, Michael. That, and the fact that Jeffries had taken a bullet that night, too. Yes, it was troubling that they hadn't been able to find the gun or a second bullet that had passed through the congressman's shoulder to test for matching ballistics, but all that did was open the possibility of an additional shooter. Or more.

What must it feel like to know that your father wanted you dead? Isaac's arms tightened around Daniella and he kissed her again, letting his lips linger before he rested his cheek against her hair.

There had to be a way to help her heart heal enough to fully trust again. And he was going to find it. No matter what he had to do.

FIFTEEN

The open door to Daniella's room kept her from feeling as if she and Isaac being together might cause his siblings to question their innocent motives. That was ridiculous, of course. The man was merely comforting her after apologizing for his gaffe about the money. And she was accepting his demonstration of friendly concern by returning his hug.

Ha-ha, her mind countered. *You may be able to fool everybody else, but don't try to fool yourself.*

She forced herself to loosen her grip and ease away from him in spite of the tender look in his eyes. Nevertheless, he released her without argument.

"Sorry," Isaac said quietly.

"For what? You didn't do anything wrong."

He shrugged. "Okay, whatever you say."

In the background a door slammed. Jacob's voice echoed up the stairwell. "I've closed and locked everything and put all the cars in the barn."

Isaac turned toward the door to answer, "Thanks."

"No problem."

He took another step away from her, leaving Daniella wishing they had remained closer. She was toying with the notion of actually saying so when she heard a familiar yip. Abby was hot on the trail of something, probably her human partner.

A smile lifted the corners of Daniella's mouth while the canine's exuberance lifted her spirits. "I think somebody is looking for you."

"Undoubtedly."

"Well…"

"Yeah, I'd better be going."

Before he had a chance to step into the hallway and shut her door, Abby barreled past in a blur of brown and white, barking all the way.

Daniella moved to try to block the dog. She may as well have tried to halt a flooded river with a teaspoon. Abby weaved past her without slowing a bit and dived under the bed!

The roar Puddy answered with was punctuated by hissing and growling.

Moving nearly as fast as the beagle, Daniella lifted the hem of the spread to peer under.

Isaac did the same.

All she could see was a flurry of tooth and claw. The combatants rolled around and around, popping out the opposite side for a moment, then back under the bed.

"Get him!" Isaac yelled. "Before he kills her."

"He's just defending himself. You grab your dog."

"I'm trying to!"

From behind them came laughter and shouts of encouragement. Jake and Becky were standing back and enjoying the melee.

Isaac didn't take his eyes off the tussle but Daniella did look up. "Help us!"

"No way. You two are doing fine." Jake guffawed.

"I've got her leg," Isaac shouted. "Pull your cat off her."

"How?"

"Grab him like his mama would, by the scruff of the neck."

The solution seemed too simplistic but she was willing to try anything at this point. She closed her fist on the loose skin behind Puddy's head and held tight while he struggled to reach the whining dog that Isaac was sliding in the opposite direction.

The cat's growling continued after the separation. Daniella began to speak soothingly to him, almost in baby talk, and he quieted in her lap, although he kept glaring at the excited beagle.

"Is Abby all right?" she asked, afraid to hear that Puddy might have injured the valuable animal.

"Yes, thankfully." Sitting on the bedroom floor, Isaac was scowling at both her and her pet. "How about your monster. Is he hurt?"

"I don't think so. Puddy was just scared because Abby showed up so unexpectedly."

"She's right," Becky offered from the doorway.

Isaac was scowling. "You would."

"I agree," Jake chimed in. "Abby's fine with the barn cats. There's no reason to believe she'd hurt this one."

Rolling his eyes, Isaac cradled his dog and watched the enormous cat. Its fur was puffed out, making it look as large as its antagonist and twice as formidable.

Abby, on the other hand, had begun to pant and drool and try to wiggle loose.

"See? She wants to be friends," Daniella said. "Put her down and see what happens."

It was evident that Isaac didn't want to follow anyone's orders, particularly hers, yet he did finally lower the dog's paws to the floor. Trembling with excitement, Abby strained against her collar and began acting like a sprinter, eager to break out of the blocks at a track meet before the starting gun fired.

Daniella offered her fingers for the beagle to sniff. "Since I was holding Puddy, this will give her an idea of what he is and calm her down."

"I didn't know you understood dogs so well.

"I get along with most animals," Daniella assured him. "A neighbor's dog was one of my best buddies when I was a kid. I wasn't allowed to have a pet of my own so I'd sneak down the street to play with Buster." Remembering more, she sobered. "I had a kitten once, when I was about seven. My dad told me it ran away and Mom suggested we not replace it. As an adult, I came to the conclusion that Dad was responsible for its disappearance."

"I'm so sorry."

"Yeah. Me, too." She shook off her doldrums and smiled while scratching behind Abby's ears. "I think you can let her loose now."

To her delight, once the dog was free, she merely stood there, sizing up her new enemy. Puddy did the same. His tail was so puffy it resembled a stiff brush.

This was the way animals met in the wild. If one felt cornered, it was natural for that one to fight. Since they were both free to advance or retreat, she believed they'd find neutral ground and call a truce.

Sure enough. Puddy made the first move, practically tiptoeing closer. One step. Two. Abby's tail began to wag and she lowered her chest to the floor, paws spread wide in a play pose, pink tongue lolling.

The cat lifted a paw and touched the dog's muzzle, then danced sideways on the tips of his toes, the end of his bushy tail beginning to twitch the way it did when Daniella dangled a toy on a string.

She held up a hand and smiled at Isaac. "Hang on. It's going to be fine."

Abby yelped.

"I think you're right. That's a play bark."

Puddy leaped, bounced off the middle of the beagle's back as if it was a trampoline, and ended up on the bed-spread.

"There. See?" Daniella said. "Now we can quit worrying about them. All is forgiven."

"Apparently." Isaac got to his feet and called his dog to heel. "I think it's time we put an end to these fun and games and all went to bed. It's late and it's been a long day."

Daniella walked him to the door, where they joined Becky and Jacob. "I still need a safe to store my money. Any suggestions?"

"I can drive you back to the bank tomorrow if you like." Becky eyed her youngest brother. "Unless Isaac wants to take you."

"I'd be glad to—right after I go interview the boy from All Our Kids foster home who witnessed the shooting at Jeffries's place."

"I thought that had been done several times," Jake said. "What else can you hope to learn?"

"I'm not sure. I've had a couple of new ideas and I'd like to ask the boy some questions myself. It may not amount to anything." He looked toward Daniella. "How about riding along with me? I'm sure I can get my captain's permission. You'll have to be blindfolded for the final few miles of the approach but it won't last long."

Smiling, she agreed. "I think I can stand doing that. Could we go to the bank first? I hate to carry all this loose cash around."

"No problem. We'll escort Becky to work in Arlington, visit your bank, then head to the safe house where the children are staying."

"Will that take you too far out of your way?" Daniella asked.

Becky caused subdued laughter when she piped up with, "Honey, I suspect my brother would go to the moon for you if you asked him to. Just take his offer of a ride and say thank you."

The grin splitting her face grew so broad her cheeks ached. Aiming it at Isaac, she repeated, "Thank you."

Isaac had decided it would be best to handle his upcoming visit to the children's home the way he had the recent one to the congressman. He'd drop in the following morning, unannounced, and trust that Cassie Danvers would be able to arrange for him to question Tommy.

He used the time trailing Becky to Arlington to mull over the details of his upcoming mission, not dreaming that his tension showed until Daniella spoke up. "Okay. Your sister is safe at her office and you're still frowning. Are you nervous about carrying all this money? You are armed, you know."

"It's not that. I'm thinking about the little boy I plan to interview."

"I can help if you'd like. I'm pretty good with kids. Most of the ones I treated in ER were either hurt or traumatized or both. They settled down fast if I kept my tone soft. They had to stop fussing in order to hear what I was saying to them."

"I guess it wouldn't hurt to let you go in with me, as long as you don't interrupt. If I need your help I'll ask for it. Okay?"

"Okay. Now suppose you tell me more about why you're wound so tight this morning."

He didn't nod but he did exhale as if he'd been holding his breath. "It's complicated."

"I'm listening."

"Cassie Danvers, housemother of All Our Kids foster home, is my captain's significant other."

"His girlfriend, you mean?"

"More than that. They're engaged. She's bound to tell him what Tommy and I talk about, especially since I plan to bring up the congressman's name."

"Why would that bother anybody?"

"Because McCord was mentored by Harland Jeffries years ago when he was a resident at the same home—and afterward, too. No matter how I handle the meeting with Tommy, it's liable to ruffle feathers. I'm already in the doghouse for pressing Jeffries about the bomb that went off near the monument."

"Their inconvenient friendship can't be helped, can it?"

Isaac huffed. "No."

"Then you have to proceed."

"Easy for you to say." He thumbed his cell phone until he'd retrieved a file of photos. "These casual pictures are what I plan to show the boy, instead of mug shots, to see if he reacts."

"And if he does?"

"Then I'll report it to my captain and take the flak, even if it costs me my job."

"Aren't you the guy who keeps telling me it's not my fault that my father was a terrible person?" She ignored his deepening scowl and continued. "Well, think about it. If McCord is one of the good guys and his buddy Jeffries is the problem, don't you think the captain will thank you for exposing a crime, no matter who's guilty?"

"It still won't be a picnic."

Daniella chuckled. "Who ever said that doing the right thing was easy? Certainly not me. So, tell me more about this children's home we're going to."

As Isaac began to fill her in on the details surrounding the attack on Cassie and the kids she cared for, he was aware that some of his apprehension was easing. It was as if Daniella's presence and empathy had infused his thoughts and helped bring peace about the difficult task he was about to undertake.

Yes, he sometimes got similar results when his team met to discuss their work, but this was different. Stronger. More defined.

He glanced over at her as he pulled up to the guarded gate that protected the safe house where the children were temporarily located. A conclusion had suddenly formed. Daniella was in the process of not only accepting a part of his job, she was getting enthusiastic about it!

It was a small, first step, Isaac realized, grateful as well as awed. Nevertheless, it was a beginning for her. For them. If she could clearly see how much it meant to him to save lives and clear the streets of criminals, perhaps she'd one day be able to tolerate the dangerous things he was called upon to do for the sake of others.

Like these innocent children, he added silently before turning his thoughts to prayer.

"Help me find the truth," Isaac whispered, circling the SUV to hold the door for his passenger. The moment his gaze lit on her face and she smiled at him, he added, "About everything."

It wasn't God's failure to hear his pleas that concerned him. It was knowing that his idea of the right answer and the Lord's actual reply might not be anywhere near the same.

Trusting Him no matter what was the hardest part.

* * *

"Aren't we taking Abby in with us?" Daniella asked, pausing before starting up the walkway to the front door.

"Not this time. There are some strange guard dogs here, helping patrol, and I don't want to risk a dogfight."

"Makes sense." She saw the front door open and two women step out. One was petite, with long reddish hair. The other was not only older, she seemed about to jump out of her skin.

Isaac took Daniella's arm and nodded to the women. "Cassie, this is a friend of mine. Daniella, meet Cassie Danvers, the foster mom I told you about, and Virginia Johnson, her helper and cook."

The redhead offered her hand. "Pleased to meet you."

"Same here." Daniella didn't even try to shake hands with the other woman for fear she'd bolt in fear. "I've worked with children before in my job as a nurse. Isaac let me come with him in case I could be of assistance."

"Nobody here is sick," Cassie insisted. Her brow knit as she focused back on Isaac. "I take it this isn't a social call?"

"I thought maybe I could have another word with Tommy."

"Don't you think he's been through enough?"

"Yes. I also think he knows more than he's told us. Like you, I want to see justice done. You and these kids can't go on living in an armed camp forever, and we don't dare let you go back to your real home until everything is solved."

It was clear to Daniella that Cassie was unsure so she stepped forward, reached for her hand again and clasped it gently. "Why don't we all go inside and discuss this?"

The housemother agreed. "All right." She gestured toward the door, where several small faces with wide eyes peeked out at her before quickly disappearing.

Daniella took special pains to smile without focusing on a particular child as she walked into the comfortable living room. There was a long sofa covered with a wrinkled throw, three small side chairs and one larger scuffed-leather one filled with what looked like hundreds of small stuffed animals.

When Cassie treated her like a valued guest and began introducing the children who were present, Daniella crouched to greet each one personally. A little waif named Rachel was the tiniest and immediately stole her heart.

"And over here is Tommy," Cassie continued, pointing to the chair with the pile of toys. "Trust me. He's bound to be under there somewhere."

A reedy, muffled voice insisted, "Uh-uh."

Smiling broadly and trying not to laugh, Daniella said, "Well, what do you know. Those animals talk!" as she perched on the matching ottoman. "My kitty talks to me sometimes, but I have trouble understanding what he says."

The pile stirred.

Daniella sat very still. "It goes like this, 'Mrrrow' or 'meorrrr,' or sometimes he hisses, but that's only when he's scared."

"I never get scared," came from the pile of animals.

"Good for you, Mr. Monkey." She picked up the closest toy and looked into its shiny black button eyes. "Or was that you, Mr. Bear?"

When the child buried under the pile of animals didn't reply, Cassie offered, "His name is Bearie."

"Good to know. My name is Daniella, Bearie."

A head of tousled, sandy-brown hair appeared amid the toys and one blue eye peeked out.

She made her reaction melodramatic, clutching the bear to her and gasping. "Oh, my." Grinning, she asked, "Are you Tommy?"

She could sense his painful shyness, see it in the way he immediately eased lower in the chair, letting only the top of his head and eyebrows show. No wonder the poor little guy was so reticent, she thought sadly. If he had witnessed the actual shooting at the congressman's estate, as Isaac believed, he'd have trouble trusting any adults. Add to that the family upheaval that had landed him in foster care in the first place, and she could easily see why he'd prefer the company of harmless stuffed toys.

Daniella held up the bear again. "I'd love to meet your friends, Bearie. Will you please introduce me?"

To her delight and surprise, Tommy's faint, childlike voice proceeded to name each stuffed animal while she held it up. She listened intently, hoping he wasn't going to ask her to repeat many of them.

"Wow, you have a really good memory, Bear. Or was that Mr. Monkey? Tell you what. Will one of you ask Tommy if he'd like to play a game with us?"

The boy's head eased out above the pile of fur, felt and stuffing, sending some of the toys sliding.

Daniella caught the closest ones. "Careful. We don't want anybody to get hurt like that poor man did who got shot. You remember seeing him, don't you, Bearie?"

The boy shook his head and averted his gaze. She'd almost lost him by going too fast. One quick glance at Isaac reassured her, so she proceeded, taking pains to guess incorrectly and thereby build up the child's confidence.

"Let me see how well I can remember something.

This is Bearie in this hand, right? And Mr. Monkey over here?"

Tommy gave her a look that indicated she was not only wrong, she wasn't too bright. Again he shook his head.

"Okay. My mistake. Now it's your turn." She took care to present a few animal toys and let the child answer for them before returning to their primary reason for visiting the home.

"Good job. I think this is too easy for all you animals. How about trying something harder?"

The spark of interest in the boy's eyes convinced her she was going to succeed this time.

Daniella lowered her voice and cupped a hand around her mouth so he had to lean closer to hear. "I know how smart you all are. You can tell good guys, like me and Officer Black over there, from bad men, can't you?"

"Uh-huh." Tommy was barely whispering.

"Good for you. How about the man with the white hair you saw that night when David's blue mitten got lost in the woods?"

Tommy retreated and drew some of the toys to his chest, where he hugged them close. "I don't wanna play."

"But how are we going to tell you won if you stop playing? Just once more, okay?" Instead of pausing to give the child time to think over his reply, she plunged ahead, holding out a hand toward Isaac and asking for his smartphone. By concentrating on its screen and hiding it from the boy, she was able to distract him again.

"Uh-uh, no peeking. I haven't found the pictures I want yet."

The first time she held up the phone for him to see, it displayed a picture of Abby.

Tommy pointed at Isaac with one of the tentacles on a green octopus. "His dog. She likes me."

"I'm sure she does." Daniella continued to work the phone, hoping she'd be able to access the file Isaac had shown her on their drive over.

"Here we go." She held up the phone with one of the pictures of a toddler Isaac had told her was named Juan.

"I know him!" In the background, Rachel clapped her hands.

"That's Juan Gomez." Cassie explained. "He used to live here."

"Right." Daniella offered Tommy a high five which he almost accepted.

Carefully paging through the photos, she found one of a smiling younger man standing beside Harland Jeffries. The only other time she'd seen an image of his son, Michael, had been in the postmortem pictures, but she wasn't about to show those to a child. If she showed this one to Tommy, there was a good chance he'd shut down again, but at least they'd know he'd seen Michael, perhaps even on the night he was shot to death.

Before turning the phone toward the boy, she held it up so Isaac could view the photo and got his silent okay.

Tommy was on his knees on the chair seat, eagerly waiting for his next test. Daniella hated to trick him but if his information cleared up the murder and freed the others in the home to return to a normal life, as Isaac hoped, it would be justified. At least she prayed it would.

Slowly pivoting, she prepared for the worst, deciding at the last minute to cover half the photo with her hand, leaving only Michael visible.

Tommy's jaw dropped. His blue eyes widened. Tears began to glisten.

Her heart broke for the frightened child. In order to reach out to him, to comfort him, Daniella had to use the hand that had masked off part of the picture.

When she did, Tommy screamed and pointed. "That's— that's the bad man with the gun!"

He burst from the pile of toys and ran straight to Cassie. She lifted his small, wiry body into her arms in spite of her diminutive size.

Daniella swallowed past the lump in her throat and stood to face Isaac, still displaying the same photo.

"He wasn't pointing to Michael Jeffries," she said with conviction. "The man he saw holding the gun was the congressman!"

Before they left the children's home, Isaac took Cassie aside and begged her to let him be the one to break the news to Gavin.

Cassie shook her head. "It will be easier for him to accept coming from me. Besides, we can't be certain Tommy is right about who was holding a gun."

Isaac gritted his teeth. He didn't want to believe the worst, either, yet couldn't help wondering. If only they could come up with a plausible motive for Michael's murder maybe the clues would start to make more sense.

"Okay, how about agreeing to give me three hours?" Isaac asked Cassie. "I should be able to get my men in place by then and find a judge willing to issue a search warrant for Jeffries's estate and office."

"Harland Jeffries founded All Our Kids foster home. He hired me. He mentored Gavin when he was an angry teenager about to go wrong. He saved him from a life on the streets and led him to the right side of the law." She took a shaky breath. "Michael was his only son. How can you even suggest he did such a horrible thing?"

Isaac was trying to come up with a valid rebuttal when Daniella stepped forward and grasped Cassie's hand.

Both women were trembling so badly he couldn't tell which was worse.

"My own father killed my mother right in front of my eyes," Daniella told Cassie, obviously speaking softly to keep from further upsetting the children. "The reason I'm with Isaac now is because my dad got out of prison and came after me. It's not unthinkable that some men might kill if they thought it was necessary for self-preservation. Maybe Harland fired by accident. Maybe he did it on purpose. Only God knows for sure."

By this time Cassie was weeping. So was Daniella. Isaac yearned to go to her and enfold her in a comforting embrace. Instead, he waited for the drama to play out.

"I'll give you two hours," Cassie finally said. "After that, I'm calling Gavin and telling him everything that happened here today."

"Fair enough." Isaac was satisfied that that was the best he could expect.

A small hand tugged at the leg of Daniella's jeans. She swiped at her cheeks and sniffled, then smiled down, surprised to see who wanted her attention. "What is it, Tommy?"

"A picture. We were swimmin'."

"I can see that. There's you, and Rachel and…" Her gasp caught Isaac's immediate notice. She was pointing at the framed photo of a group of small children in a wading pool. "Who's this?"

Tommy grew solemn. "That's Juan. I wish he'd come back. He likes my animals."

Straightening, Daniella showed the picture to Cassie, then to Isaac. "Do you see a faint birthmark on this boy's shoulder or am I imagining things?"

"He had a good-size mark on his back, near the shoulder," Cassie said. "It was kind of hard to see against his darker skin but it was there, all right."

"Café au lait," Daniella murmured. She stared at the other woman. "Was Michael Jeffries his father?"

Cassie shook her head emphatically.

"How can you be so sure?"

"Because, Michael wrote an article for the Washington Post promoting adoption, and confessed he couldn't have kids of his own."

Isaac cupped Daniella's elbow to turn and guide her toward the exit. He didn't want to waste one second of his two-hour window, so he exerted gentle pressure. "We really do have to go. I'll bring you back later if you want and you ladies can have a good cry together."

They were seated in the SUV before Daniella responded with words. She blotted her damp cheeks first, then said, "We don't choose to cry, Isaac. Our female brains make more of the natural chemicals that cause us to weep than men's brains do."

"I've seen guys lose it," he countered.

"Yes, but it usually takes a lot more to bring a man to tears than it does to affect a woman the same way. It's not a weakness, it's the way God made us."

"And He never makes mistakes, right?"

"Right. Seeing a woman's tears has a tendency to also alter a normal male's brain chemistry and make him more sympathetic."

"Humph."

What he wanted to do was counter her claim with a macho comment that would disprove that hypothesis. He could not. Truth to tell, his own emotions had been affected by seeing the women so upset, particularly Daniella. He had brought her to the foster home and allowed her to become involved in his work again. He should have known better.

There was no question that he could control his emotions. After all, he'd already seen plenty of suffering and there was undoubtedly more waiting in his future. What he could not deny, however, was the tugging at his heart and the boulder that sat in the pit of his stomach every time he saw joy leave Daniella's face.

She might never know the entire truth, but he did. There was not a shadow of a doubt.

Her pain was his. It always would be.

Instead of relying on the earwig, Isaac picked up the mic, identified his unit and told the dispatcher to switch to another channel while Daniella sat in the passenger seat and listened.

"I have a credible witness to the shooting at the Jeffries estate and a probable motive for Rosa Gomez's murder, too, when we get time to look into it," he reported. "I'll need a search warrant for Harland Jeffries's property and a task force assembled ASAP." He paused. "One more thing. This is vital. Do your notifications by cell or in person. Do not let Captain McCord find out what we're doing if you can possibly help it."

The voice on the radio said, "That's against protocol."

"I know. I left an urgent message for General Meyer, and I'll brief her as soon as she calls me back. If anybody gives you trouble, tell them to check with her and mention my name."

Daniella could tell he was really torn by having to act behind McCord's back. "Maybe it would be best to tell the captain before Cassie's two hours are up," she suggested when he was finished on the radio. "He has a right to know everything, even if the suspect is an old friend of his, and that way you can express your conclusions so he'll be more likely to understand."

"No. I don't want to take a chance on being stopped until we've searched the congressman's house and grounds."

"What are you hoping to find? Surely he wouldn't have kept clues around if he did shoot his son."

"Probably not. I suppose the shooter could just as easily have been Erin Eagleton, like most people thought. Tommy didn't say he saw Harland actually pull the trigger."

"The trick is going to be convincing him to speak up and comment more on that night without putting any notions into his head. Kids can be very impressionable."

"That's what I figured. By the way, thanks for your help. I never thought of making my interrogation into a game the way you did."

"You're welcome." The compliment warmed her to the core and brought a slight smile. "I don't want the poor kid to be scarred for life because of seeing something awful, but I do wish he hadn't run away before the actual shooting."

"Yeah, if that's what he really did."

Driving back to DC, they approached the hospital where Daniella had worked and she felt a pang of nostalgia. No matter how trying her job had been at times, she'd enjoyed doing it. She was about to comment along those lines when Isaac's cell phone sounded.

"Maybe that's your big boss returning your call."

"I hope so."

She saw his face change when he looked at the ID on the small screen. "Becky? What's wrong?"

Daniella didn't have to hear the answer to know it was something dire. Isaac clenched his jaw muscle. His eyes narrowed. He pulled to the shoulder of the road just before they reached the beltway and handed his phone to her.

"Becky?" she said, wishing they were together so she could read her friend's face as well as she was reading Isaac's. When the connection stayed quiet, she pleaded, "Talk to me. Please?"

The sound of shuffling in the background was all that was coming through. Then she heard what had to be a slap, a gasp and a thud, followed by a shaky "Daniella?"

Clearly there was something terribly wrong. Cradling the small cell phone, she motioned to Isaac to shut off the SUV's engine so she could hear every nuance.

When Becky did start to speak, it was rapid-fire and barely understandable. "Kidnapped. Don't come after me. I'm…"

Again there was the smacking sound of flesh against flesh and then a scream. "No!"

The evil-sounding cackle that followed made Daniella physically ill. She held out the phone and stared at it rather than keeping it pressed to her ear. One look at Isaac told her he already knew who had taken his sister.

Becky was with someone even worse than Harland Jeffries was suspected of being.

She'd been abducted by Terence Fagan!

Isaac reclaimed his phone. "Where's my sister, you useless…?"

"Now, now, is that any way to talk in front of a lady?"

"What do you want?"

"A simple trade," Fagan said. "My woman for yours."

"No trade. We don't negotiate with kidnappers."

"In that case, say goodbye to your sister."

"Wait." He eyed Daniella, looking for a sign of approval

as he said, "How about a ransom? Your daughter has a lot of money stashed away."

She was nodding rapidly, clearly in agreement, and leaned closer to Isaac to put her ear next to his and eavesdrop on the conversation.

Fagan chuckled. "It's a tad too late for that. I'm afraid this conversation is over. If you won't trade my daughter for your sister, she's of no use to me anymore."

Shouting "Wait" into the phone, Daniella tried to wrest it from Isaac. He held fast so she resorted to yelling. "I'll come. I'll take her place. I promise I will. Just don't hurt her."

"No, she won't," Isaac insisted, pulling away and stepping out of the car to distance himself from her interference. Pacing, he continued to argue with Fagan, hoping the man would listen to reason or at least be tempted by the big payday Daniella could provide.

"I figure it must be close to half a million," Isaac told him. "I can get it and deliver it to you. Just tell me where and when."

"I thought you didn't negotiate."

"Officially, we don't."

"But my having your sister makes a difference?"

"Yes." It galled him to admit weakness, yet he had no choice. The only way to rescue Becky was to stall her kidnapper until he could set a trap for him, probably at the site of the exchange. As long as Fagan kept him busy on the phone he couldn't arrange a thing. Not a thing.

Isaac motioned for Daniella to join him and once again shared the phone with her.

She clapped a hand over her opposite ear. "What? I can't hear you."

"Where's the cop?"

"He's right here. We both are."

Isaac affirmed her claim, making a rolling motion with one hand to indicate she should keep talking and stall. Then he slipped back into the SUV to radio headquarters and inform them of the kidnapping. He was taking a chance by trying to trick a wily criminal like Fagan. Daniella's wits were going to have to keep them both out of hot water.

He laid down the mic when he saw her motioning wildly for him to return to her.

"Noise is bad here. Say again?" Isaac asked. His heart fell when he heard Fagan's demand.

"Look, I can't get home that fast. We were headed back to DC. We're clear on the opposite side of the beltway right now and traffic is almost at a standstill."

"Excuses? You don't want your sister back, do you?"

"Of course I do." The phone cackled as if it had a mind of its own, and the hair on the back of Isaac's neck prickled.

"I'll give you one hour to get back to your farm," Fagan told Isaac. "Any longer than that and your sister dies." Another laugh grated. "And when you call your brother to tip him off, make sure he understands that I'll be ready to put a bullet in her the second I think something's wrong, so he'd better behave himself."

"Why rendezvous at the farm?" Isaac asked. "Why didn't you just blow up the house with the last bomb and get it over with?" Dead silence on the other end of the line was confusing.

Finally, Fagan spoke. "I don't know what you're trying to pull, but I didn't have time to place explosives at your house when I was there. I was too busy shooting at my ungrateful kid. Almost got her, too. And you and your buddies and those ugly mutts."

Before Isaac could question him further, Fagan added, "Look at your watch and get moving. The hour starts now."

Grabbing Daniella's arm and half dragging her with him, he raced for the car. "Hurry. We only have an hour to get home and I have a lot of preparations to make in the meantime."

"Do you want me to drive?"

"Only if you've had a defensive driving course."

She climbed in the passenger side and slammed her door, then reached for the buckle ends of the seat belt. "Can we make it?"

He flicked on the lights and siren and eased away from the curb. Most of the passing cars gave him the right-of-way as soon as they could find a place to pull over— which wasn't easy.

In the clear, Isaac floored the accelerator. They'd get home in under an hour. They had to.

The only thing he didn't like was keeping Daniella with him. If he could think of any safe place to drop her, or imagined for one second that she'd stay out of trouble on her own, he'd gladly leave her standing at the curb and speed off.

One glance at her determined expression and the way she was clenching her fists told him they must stay together. Leaving her to her own devices, the way she had been when she'd driven her car into the path of rifle bullets, was out of the question. He didn't know how he was going to control her once she saw her father and Becky. He simply knew he had to try.

And keep trying.

Until there were no more chances left.

SIXTEEN

Daniella didn't think this was a good time to mention that Isaac's erratic driving was making her carsick, so she bit her lip and endured.

Radio traffic had come at them so fast she was pretty confused. Not that it mattered. She'd do whatever Isaac told her to do. She clenched her jaw and amended that promise. Common sense had to take precedence over orders if there was no doubt he needed her help.

She was about to ask him what her role was to be when he turned to her and explained. "Jake is going to be upstairs, out of sight, when we arrive. He'll be armed with the .12 gauge shotgun. That will mean he can't make distance shots but it'll be fine for defense if it comes to that. Unless he calls to tell us Fagan beat us to the farm, I want you to make a run for the house as soon as we get there and head straight for Jake. He'll protect you. Got that?"

"Yes." Daniella's mouth was so dry she could hardly swallow. Her immediate goal had to be a facade of calm, for Isaac's sake if not for her own.

"Culpeper police are already on scene. They know about Jake and to watch for this vehicle."

"So they don't shoot us?"

"Ideally, yes," Isaac said, grimacing. "I'd prefer to

have men I've worked with backing me up but they're still fifteen minutes out. If we wait for them…"

"We may be too late to save Becky."

"Exactly."

Daniella could tell how concerned Isaac was, and the guilt piled on top of her like tons of sand being unloaded from a dump truck. No matter how hard she tried to rationalize, this kidnapping and whatever followed was her fault. When she'd had a chance to hit the road again and hadn't followed through, she'd made things worse.

In view of how hard her companion was concentrating and the speed of his driving, she decided to keep any negative thoughts to herself. Isaac needed to focus on freeing his sister. Period.

Yes, she would run upstairs and join Jake. And, yes, she would stay out of the way while the police surrounded her father and made him surrender. But if things started to look bad for Isaac, Becky and Jacob, she was *not* going to stand idly by and observe.

As far as Daniella was concerned, the plan of trading her for Becky was viable. Terence Fagan was not going to win. Not if she had anything to say about it.

"I don't see the cops," Isaac muttered, wheeling into the driveway and barely slowing until he reached the sheltered area next to the barn.

"They're supposed to be hiding," Daniella reminded him.

"There should be an officer I can talk to, somebody who can brief me on their plans."

"Shall I wait?" she asked.

Isaac's "No!" was gruff and loud. He tempered his anxiety as best he could and pointed at the back door. "Sorry. Just go."

If this had been a regular assignment, not involving his loved ones, he'd have carried out his orders with calm assurance and technical expertise. For the first time since the academy, he could understand why agents who were personally involved with a situation were pulled off that case. Knowing the victims too well did change a person's reactions and hamper judgment.

With no sign of Fagan or Becky and the knowledge that the other man may have been within viewing range of them in the city, Isaac assumed he'd arrived first. Therefore, it made sense to use Abby one more time, just in case. Fagan's choice of the farm as a meeting place seemed odd. In case he'd already been there and planted explosives again, hoping to get rid of all of them at once, this was the ideal time to conduct a quick sweep.

He released his dog, then started to work his way around the house. Jake would take care of Daniella, he would face Fagan and get Becky back, and the police, wherever they were, would take the convicted felon into custody.

That was how it all worked in textbooks. Right now, Isaac would have agreed to any scenario that would bring his loved ones out alive.

He pictured Daniella and took a deep breath, releasing it with a whoosh. Yes. His loved ones. *All* of them.

"How long have you been up here?" Daniella asked Jacob.

"Since Isaac called."

"You've been able to watch the road that whole time?"

Jake nodded. "Yeah."

"Have you seen any local cops?"

"A patrol car cruised through the yard, then left. Either they didn't understand what was going down or they decided it wasn't important. I ran downstairs to talk to them but they were already gone."

"Didn't you report it?"

"Oh, sure. And whoever took my call acted as if I was overreacting." He snorted derisively. "Apparently they were expecting to drive up and see a gunfight. When the place was quiet, they thought the threat was over."

"Are they coming back?"

He shrugged. "They said they were but I sure haven't seen any sign of them."

"What are we going to do?" She grabbed his forearm. "We can't leave Isaac down there all alone to face my dad. What about Becky?"

He laid a warm, strong hand over hers. "Look. I know you want to help, but we won't do Isaac any favors if we get in his way and mess up his plans."

"Ha! I listened to him making plans on the drive home. It sounded more like the script for a sitcom. He won't know what to do until he sees Becky and that awful man."

"At least, thanks to Abby, we'll be sure there's no bomb this time."

"Big whoop. Where there are bullets, who needs a stupid bomb?"

Knowing Jake didn't deserve her sarcasm, she reined it in. "Sorry. I'm getting to the end of my rope. I didn't mean to take it out on you."

"Holler all you want," he told her with a slight smile. "Believe me, I've felt like it today."

"I'm going down the hall to use the restroom," Daniella said. "Be right back."

The fact that Jake let her leave his side without complaint proved that he believed her. And she hadn't lied, exactly. She was going to splash cold water on her face from the bathroom sink. Her only secret was she didn't intend to go back to him before checking on a couple of other things.

She glanced at her watch. Less than ten minutes until the meeting. Everything would soon be over.

And, God willing, the good guys would win.

A nagging voice in the recesses of her brain kept asking, *What if they don't?*

That premise was unacceptable. She didn't have a gun as Becky did and wouldn't have known how to use it if she had. Knives were also out. After helping care for victims of knife fights, she knew she'd never be able to hurt anyone that way. Besides, she'd have to get too close, and anybody with a gun could cut her down before she had a chance.

So what was left? Visions of armored knights on horseback wielding lances led her toward the familiar kitchen. In medieval days, castle defenders had dropped burning logs or poured pots of boiling oil down on their enemies. That would work only if her foes happened to stand below one of the upstairs windows, but she figured it was better to prepare *something* than to stand there like a lamb waiting for slaughter.

Isaac was no longer visible in the yard. There was no sign of her father and Becky yet, either. Live coals were out because they might ignite the whole house. Would she have time to get a pot of cooking oil hot enough to burn someone?

There was only one way to find out. She turned on a burner, grabbed a pan and started to fill it with corn oil. Watching it heat, she berated herself for trying such a silly idea. She would gladly have done something else, something far more clever, if anything had come to mind.

Most of all, she yearned to know the unknowable, that they were all going to survive. Closing her eyes, Daniella turned to the only source of comfort available. She took her heartfelt appeal to the One who was always there, always faithful, her heavenly Father.

This time there was no sense of peace, no unusual result, no amazing realization. This time, she saw that part of the answer was up to her. First, she must trust the Lord of the universe. Then, she must employ the wits He had given her and be ready to act in whatever manner He presented. Bravely. Quickly. Without thought for self-preservation.

Was she afraid to risk her life? Of course she was. But she needed to take part in the rescue in order to redeem herself. How that might happen was yet to be determined.

Peering out the window over the kitchen sink, her breath caught. Isaac had returned and was standing firm, feet apart, one hand hovering over his holstered gun like a sheriff in an old Western.

A green van fishtailed around the corner, heading straight for him.

He never flinched.

Clamping her hands over her mouth, Daniella stifled a scream. She could not move, could not force herself to look away. Not even if...

The tires of the green vehicle threw up clouds of dust as it slid to a halt mere inches from the K-9 cop.

Round one to Isaac, she thought with heart-stopping relief. Should she stay where she was and continue watching, praying, or should she grab the hot pan of oil and take it upstairs?

That question was answered when she saw her estranged father climb from the van. He hauled a bruised, disheveled Becky out after him, wrenching her past the steering wheel as if she were of no consequence, and pointing toward the house.

Daniella realized she'd run out of time. If she'd gone back to Jake sooner she'd already be in place with the oil, ready to pour it on Fagan.

Instead, she turned and raced up the stairs, calling herself all sorts of names for not acting promptly enough. What good was a weapon if she wasn't in the right position to use it?

On the second floor again, she tiptoed to the rear bedroom, where she'd last seen Jacob, and soundlessly pushed open the door.

She froze. Her feet felt glued to the floor.

Jacob—and his shotgun—were gone!

The kitchen door slammed.

Becky gave a muffled cry of pain as she was shoved into a chair.

Isaac spun around, reaching for his sister, and felt a sharp pain slice through his temple.

He dropped to his knees, dazed.

If it hadn't been for Fagan's pistol and his sister's vulnerability, he would have jumped the older man outside. "Where's my rich little girl?" Fagan drawled.

Still kneeling, Isaac raised up, supported by one arm while the other probed his scalp wound. "I told you the money was in Arlington. If you wanted it, you should have met us there."

"Naw. My Ella and I can pick it up later. Or I can go by myself after she tells me which bank it's in."

"She put it in a safe-deposit box," Isaac informed him, hoping that news would help keep the hostages alive a little longer, himself included.

"Think you're smart, don't ya?" Fagan wielded the pistol like a club, barely missing Isaac's forehead when he swung this time.

That error left him a fraction off balance. His arms cartwheeled.

Isaac rocketed up off the floor and hit him squarely in the midsection. They both staggered backward.

Becky was too battered to do more than raise one foot and trip her captor as he passed.

That, coupled with Isaac's weight, was enough to down him and send the gun sliding away across the smooth vinyl.

Fagan writhed, twisted, stretched toward his pistol.

A shrill "No!" echoed through the house and into the kitchen. If Fagan recognized the woman's voice, he gave no indication of it. Isaac, however, knew exactly who was shouting.

"Get out of here," he yelled, breathless from grappling with her nefarious father and angry that she would so blatantly disobey a sensible order.

"Becky, grab the gun!" Daniella screeched from the foot of the stairs.

Fagan's straining fingers brushed the pistol grip too hard and pushed the gun farther away instead of capturing it.

Isaac saw a flash of movement as someone dashed past and for a moment thought the stubborn nurse was going to follow his instructions to flee.

That instant of inattention was nearly fatal. The man he'd had pinned to the kitchen floor threw himself sideways and flipped Isaac onto his back, grabbing his wrists and holding them immobile, keeping either of them from getting to the loose pistol.

Isaac had a holdout gun in an ankle holster he couldn't reach. His quarry, being heavier and having a clear head, had gained the advantage. His sister was groggier than he was, and to make terrible matters worse, Daniella was somewhere nearby.

Didn't she know how dangerous it was for her? Hadn't she seen enough of her father's deeds to guess what he'd do to her the first chance he got?

Struggling mightily, Isaac raised his shoulders off the floor, preparing to head-butt Fagan, even if it knocked them both out.

A primal roar from above and slightly behind made him freeze. There was a flash of metal. A swish of air. Followed by a hollow-sounding *bonk* that reminded him of the time Jake had dropped a ripe watermelon on their mother's living room carpet.

Fagan slumped forward, unconscious.

Pushing the man's limp body off his chest, Isaac struggled to his feet, expecting to see that his brother had come to his rescue.

Instead, Daniella stood off to one side, armed with a cast-iron skillet that was older than their combined ages. Her muscles were quivering and her eyes enormous. Nevertheless, she had taken the stance needed to repeat the blow and was clearly ready to do so.

"I'll take that," Isaac told her, stopping to scoop up Fagan's gun.

His other fist closed around the handle of the skillet. Daniella released it so easily he almost fumbled. "What did you think you were doing?"

"Saving your life." She leaned past Isaac to look at her father. "Did I kill him?"

"No, honey. I imagine you gave him a corker of a headache, though." He guided her to a chair and urged her to sit so he could turn his attention to his sister.

Becky looked black-and-blue but she was also grinning at Daniella. "Good one. If I wasn't so whipped right now I'd borrow your pan and give him a whack myself."

Isaac glanced at the prone figure. Fagan hadn't moved a muscle but was breathing regularly. "Looks like he'll be out for a while. I'll cuff him, anyway." He reached for his duty belt before recalling that he'd been forced to drop it outside after he'd been relieved of his weapon, as well.

The sound of distant sirens was rapidly growing louder so Isaac opted to tend to his injured sister for a few more moments. Rinsing a dishcloth in cold water, he folded it and laid it on her forehead. "Better?"

"Mmm, thanks. That feels good." She closed her eyes and sighed.

Daniella was also concerned with Becky's condition. "We need antiseptic and gauze squares to clean her cuts and scrapes. She should see a doctor, too, as soon as possible."

"We'll let the EMTs handle those details." He straightened, glancing toward the unconscious man and expecting to see the same scene as before.

Instead, he watched as Terence Fagan stood. He was brandishing a different weapon—the gun he'd taken from Isaac when he'd first arrived at the farm.

Isaac shouted, "Look out!"

Becky screamed.

Daniella ricocheted off the edge of the kitchen counter, unsuccessfully trying to thwart her father's attempt to grab her.

Isaac had pulled his reliable holdout gun, but Daniella was in the way of a clean shot.

All he could do was stand there and watch as Fagan dragged her, kicking and screaming, across the kitchen toward the back door.

SEVENTEEN

In Daniella's mind she'd been captured by the most evil person in the entire world. Every fiber of her being raged against his touch. Her wrist ached and her skin burned where his fingers were clamped. Screams filled her throat, erupting in a cacophony of earsplitting wailing accompanied by a degree of physical resistance far beyond her normal strength.

Bracing herself, she labored to gain traction. Her gaze raked the room, searching for any weapon or means of escape, while her soles skidded on the vinyl.

The stove! Could she reach it? Every second took her a little farther away. She lunged, jerking until her captive arm gave with a pop and she suspected she'd dislocated her shoulder.

No amount of pain was enough to stop her. Not when she was so close. Panic muted the worst of the pulsing agony, allowing her to continue to strain. So close. So very close. Her extended fingers trembled with the effort. Another inch. That's all she needed. Just one more try. She could last that long. She had to.

A groan started low in her throat, emerging with an urgency that fit her fight for life better and better as the pitch and volume rose, surprising even her.

Fagan's grip relaxed very slightly. That was enough. Daniella twisted. *Free!*

Her fist closed on the handle of the pan of oil. She didn't stop to wonder if the contents were hot enough to do damage. She just swung.

Centrifugal force carried the pan in an arc toward Fagan and left a trail of spilled oil in its wake.

Daniella continued to attack. The pan failed to make contact with the man's head, as she'd hoped, but the hot oil splashed across his face and chest.

Both arms flew up to shield his eyes, temporarily destroying any opportunity for an accurate shot.

Seeing her chance, Daniella prepared for another swing. Off to her left, she saw Isaac taking aim. She thought she heard him bark an order to her, but Fagan's screeching and cursing made it too hard to hear.

He had pivoted away and was scrambling for the door, slipping on the oily floor. Common sense pulled her the opposite way in spite of a burning desire to keep after him, to make sure he was captured and put back in prison where he belonged.

"Stop or I'll shoot," Isaac roared.

Terence Fagan ignored the warning. He jerked open the door and stumbled out, raising his firearm in front of him as he did so.

A loud bang shook the windows. Fagan's body was driven backward off the porch as if he'd been lassoed around the waist by a giant and given a mighty yank.

Frozen in place, Daniella saw plenty through the doorway. She didn't know what kind of weapon had made the booming sound, but she could guess. Jake must have left the house and sneaked around to find a better vantage point. When her father had aimed the pistol at him, he'd shot first.

Shouts outside mingled with those of the uniformed officers who burst into the kitchen. Some were local cops but the majority wore the patches and gear of Isaac's K-9 unit. Most had their dog partners by their sides.

At this point, Daniella wanted nothing more than to be in Isaac's arms regardless of who might see them together and question his motives. He welcomed her with open arms.

"Is—is he dead?" Daniella asked.

"Medics are checking him," Isaac told her. "He probably is."

She clung to him, listening to the rapid pounding of his heart and wondering why she felt so odd.

He gently stroked her back and murmured his support. "Are you okay?"

Raising her face to look directly into his eyes and draw more comfort, she nodded. "It's very confusing."

"What is?"

"My feelings. My reactions. I thought I'd be overjoyed when that man died, but I'm almost sad. That makes absolutely no sense. He tried to kill me. I should be happier now. What's wrong with me?"

"Not a thing." Isaac bent to kiss her lightly on the forehead. "I wondered if you'd stay bitter after all the horrible things he did to you and your mother. I'm glad to see you were able to forgive him enough to go on with your life. Hate can cripple a person as badly as a broken bone."

"Hmm." He was right, of course. And nobody was more surprised by her tempered attitude than she was. The emotional roller coaster might not be over yet, but Isaac was right. She could see an end to the grudge she'd been holding and the undeserved guilt that had accompanied it.

Settling against him with her arms wrapped around

his waist, she wished they could stay that way indefinitely. It was the aching, prickling soreness of her shoulder that snapped her out of that lovely daydream.

"When the paramedics are done with Becky, I'd like one of them to take a look at my arm and shoulder. I may have dislocated something in the struggle."

"Why didn't you say so?"

Daniella looked up at him, touched by his evident concern. "Because you were hugging me and I didn't want that to end," she whispered for his ears only. "I really like it."

Isaac arched a brow, his dark eyes glistening. "Me, too. Do you think that might be another good sign?"

Because they were surrounded by officers and dogs, she cupped a hand around her mouth to speak aside. "I think it's definitely worth discussing, preferably in private."

"*After* we get your injuries looked at," Isaac said firmly.

"You are one bossy cop, you know that?"

"I think you're up to the challenge, don't you?"

If the atmosphere in the room had not been so somber she would have smiled, although it seemed wrong to even consider doing so. Not only were her thoughts scrambled, her emotions were, too. What she needed to do—what they all needed to do—was calm down and process everything slowly and sensibly.

Daniella was already positive she loved Isaac in spite of his job. The notion that he might love her in return made her giddy.

So which was it to be? she asked herself. *Do I let myself admit how much I care and face the threat of losing him every time he goes to work, or do I listen to my cowardly side and push him away?*

There had been a time, not many days before, when

she would have let her fears govern her choices. Today, having repeatedly cheated death and survived, she was far less certain.

"What do you mean you found another bomb?" Isaac could hardly believe his ears.

The rookie officer looked very pleased with himself. "No lie. We nabbed the perp red-handed. Might have missed him if a cute little dog hadn't flushed him out of the bushes."

"A beagle? With a playful attitude?"

"Sounds about right, except she wasn't acting playful when she latched on to the guy's ankle."

Isaac smiled. "Abby's actually a police dog but she's trained to use her nose, not her teeth. She must have been watching the attack dogs being worked."

"Well, wherever she learned the trick, it worked."

Hesitant to leave the scene, even for a few minutes, Isaac glanced over at the blue plastic sheet covering Fagan's body, then at the nearby ambulance where Daniella and Becky were being treated. Fagan had seemed genuinely surprised when he'd insisted he hadn't placed the previous device in the farmhouse basement. Was it possible he'd had an accomplice? If that man had decided to take matters into his own hands, it was a good thing he'd been captured or they'd still be in jeopardy.

"Take me to your suspect," Isaac ordered.

When he rounded the house with the other officer, his jaw dropped. Captain McCord was standing next to a patrol car, holding Abby in his arms. The handcuffed prisoner beside him was dressed like any other rural worker, but that was where the similarity ended. Isaac recognized him instantly. It was Leon Ridge, one of Congressman Jeffries's aides!

Struggling to make sense of what he was seeing, Isaac frowned at his captain. "What's Leon doing here?"

"That's a good question," McCord replied, passing Abby to her partner. "He's not talking."

"I was told there was a bomber in custody."

Nodding, McCord pointed to a shoe box that was currently being examined by a team of experts wearing heavy protective suits. "According to your dog, there is. Leon was caught trying to slip that into your basement through the coal chute. Since that's how the last bomb was delivered, we assume that's what's in this box, too."

As Isaac puzzled over the proof, he saw a member of the bomb disposal unit wave.

Leon Ridge spoke up. "Hey, I'm just an innocent bystander. A guy named Fagan left that. I happened to see him do it and just wanted to take a look."

Turning to his captain, Isaac shook his head emphatically. "Impossible. Fagan took my sister from work in Arlington, then hung around DC to make contact with me because he was after Daniella. There's no way he had time or opportunity to place another bomb."

Ridge shouted, "I saw him, I tell you," while one of the local officers secured him in the rear of the closest patrol car.

"If I hadn't been so worried about Becky I'd already have a report on your desk," Isaac told McCord. "Daniella and I talked with Tommy Benson this morning." He hesitated, wishing he didn't have to be the one to tell his boss about Tommy's identification of the congressman.

"And?"

"I'd rather think it through and type it up for you."

The captain huffed. "Yeah. I have an idea I'd rather not hear it, either, but lay it on me. We may as well bring everything out in the open, starting with the lab finding Leon's prints on the first bomb we took out of your basement."

"Jeffries!" Isaac was astounded.

"I've had my suspicions about Harland for some time. Finding Leon here confirms them, although I can't understand why he'd send an aide to frame Fagan and do away with you."

"Yeah, there is that." Isaac was shaking his head as some of the pieces of the puzzle fell into place. "Jeffries must have gone over the edge. No totally sane person would think that eliminating me would stop any of his secrets from getting out." He paused before saying, "Tommy said he saw Harland pointing a handgun at Michael the night of the murder."

"That still doesn't explain who shot Harland."

"Doesn't it?" Isaac nodded at the prisoner waiting in the patrol car. "Leon is his fixer. I think, once we get through interrogating him, we'll know if Harland's crazy enough to tell somebody to put a bullet in him just to keep from looking guilty."

To Isaac's surprise, the captain said, "Now that I'm beginning to see the whole picture, I think he just might be. He's definitely in over his head."

"Don't forget Rosa Gomez. Leon or another of the congressman's aides may have done away with her, too." Isaac paused. "I think it's highly possible Harland ordered her killed, especially if we're right about Juan's birthmark being inherited from Harland instead of Michael."

"I suppose that's part of another unwritten report?"

"Yes." Isaac filled in his captain about Juan Gomez having the same birthmark as Michael and Harland Jeffries, that Michael was reportedly unable to have children and that Harland Jeffries was very likely Juan

Gomez's father. Isaac could see his captain's mind working—that Harland may have had Juan's mother killed to keep her quiet since an "illegitimate" child from an affair with his housekeeper would have hurt his chances for reelection.

What was less clear was why Harland would kill his own son. What was the motive there?

Since little Tommy didn't see Harland Jeffries pull the trigger, and since Harland had been shot, too, the Capitol K-9 Unit still had more questions than answers. What they did know for sure was that Harland Jeffries wasn't the man everyone thought he was.

Isaac laid a hand of comfort and support on Gavin McCord's shoulder. "I'm sorry."

"Yeah," the captain replied, "me, too."

"Please, let me go with you?"

"Don't you want to hang around here and nurse Becky?"

"She's sleeping and Jake is watching over her. There's no reason for me to stay here when I can go with you."

"You could mop the kitchen floor."

"I've done that twice and we're out of grease-cutting detergent. Try again."

"You'd be bored silly. Trust me, it's not the way you see it on TV. There's very little excitement at police stations." Isaac smiled at Daniella and slipped an arm around her shoulders, using a light touch where a sling supported her left arm. "How are you feeling?"

"Frustrated and tense," she answered.

"Why? The danger's over."

"For me, maybe. You're still in somebody's sights. If I stay behind while you go into the city, I'll worry myself sick."

"So, what else is new?"

She took a playful swing at him. "That's not what I mean. We both know my father couldn't have been responsible for everything. With the congressman's aide in custody, you may find out enough to tell who's behind the rest of the terrible things that have been happening."

"And we may not. Leon's a pro at lying. After all, politics is a good teacher."

Daniella quieted and made a decision that would probably affect her whole future. At least she hoped it would. She looked up at Isaac, reveling in the way he gazed back at her and astounded by how rapidly her heart had opened to him.

"Okay. Let me put it this way. I thought I was going to die when my father tried to drag me away from you. Then I thought we might *all* be out of time, which was even worse."

When Isaac opened his mouth to speak, she stilled him by placing her fingertips on his lips.

"Let me finish. Please?"

He assented.

"I used to think I'd never consider falling for anybody like you, no matter how attracted I was."

"Are you saying…?"

"Hush!" Daniella's growing smile mirrored the joy she was seeing on his face. "What I'm saying right now is that I do not want to be away from you for even a second. It may not make much sense, but that's the way I feel."

"You just lost a parent. Naturally you'd look for an anchor."

"Ha! The only anchor my father would have considered providing is one he could tie around my ankle right before throwing me overboard. It's not that, Isaac. It's you. And me. And if you won't let me ride along with you this time, I'll throw a hissy fit that will curl your hair."

"Is that so?"

"Try me."

Instead of being angry at the threat, he started to laugh and pulled her into his embrace. "I'd love to see you revert to acting like the younger kids at the foster home, but your tantrum will have to wait."

"We're going?" If her shoulder hadn't been throbbing, she'd have jumped up and down.

"We're going. Together. Grab your purse and meet me at the SUV. I'll go tell Jake I'm taking you with me and pick up Abby."

Daniella assured herself she couldn't have been happier if he'd dropped to one knee and proposed. That thought stopped her in midstride. Her decision to admit feelings of affection hadn't gone quite that far.

She knew she wanted desperately to be near Isaac. Being away from him caused true pangs of longing and made him seem so appealing, so amazingly right for her, that it took her breath away. Was that love? Was it enough?

More important, would it be enough for the rest of their lives? She didn't want to commit to anything until she was sure. So, how long would that take—and would she recognize it if and when it occurred?

Daniella grabbed her purse, gathering the strap in her hand rather than chance bumping her sore shoulder, and proceeded to the K-9 unit vehicle.

The yard was empty, as if the earlier mayhem had never occurred. Her glance kept returning to focus on the door. Watching. Waiting.

It swung open. Abby nosed out ahead of Isaac. A grin split Daniella's face and her heart leaped the moment she laid eyes on him. Yearning built within her until she could hardly contain her exuberance.

His eyes met hers. He smiled that amazing smile she so adored, and it was meant for only her.

No more questions remained. She loved Isaac Black. That was all there was to it.

Instead of climbing into the passenger seat on her own, Daniella paused until he'd secured Abby in the rear compartment and looked for her.

"Need some help?"

"Yes, please. My arm hurts," she said, which was the truth as far as it went.

Isaac approached. Opened and held the door.

Daniella tossed her purse in first, then slipped her uninjured arm around her hero's neck and stood on tiptoe to kiss him gently.

His lips softened. He slid an arm around her waist, lifted and steadied her, as he deepened the kiss.

That ideal response was all the proof she needed. Isaac loved her. Now all she had to do was convince herself to accept that unexpected gift and adjust her plans accordingly, which might be tough to do after spending the past ten years insisting she was perfectly content to spend the rest of her life alone.

To Daniella's astonishment and dismay, she discovered it was far easier to fall in love in the first place than it was to deal with the changes that that love might be bringing.

Isaac seemed to tremble slightly as he set her away and guided her into the SUV.

When she tried to fasten her seat belt one-handed and failed, she realized that most of the unsteadiness was coming from her.

And when he reached across the seat to secure her belt

for her and their fingers brushed, she wondered if it was possible her anatomy instructors had been wrong when they'd taught that bones were so strong.

She was positive hers were about to melt.

EIGHTEEN

It didn't surprise Isaac that the interrogation of Leon Ridge was lengthy. It took hours of constant questioning before Ridge caved and implicated the congressman at all. When he did, questions about corruption and taking bribes were answered and some suspicions confirmed, but law enforcement was far from done grilling Leon.

Although they now had a plausible motive for Rosa's murder, namely Juan and his birthmark, they were still working on the details of Michael's shooting death. All Leon Ridge would admit was his part in the wounding of Harland Jeffries and he claimed that had happened after Michael was already dead. The fact that Erin Eagleton's name was also mentioned bothered Isaac, yes, but nowhere near as much as it bothered Chase Zachary, another member of the K-9 team, who was better acquainted with her.

After Daniella's first trip to headquarters, she had quit asking to go along again, much to Isaac's relief. The hardest part for him was seeing her at home with his siblings and not picturing her as part of the family. He'd hinted about it over and over, trying to judge her level of commitment and ending up more confused instead.

She was an enigma; one day kissing him as if she were

head over heels in love and the next treating him with no more casual affection than she displayed toward his brother and sister.

Becky counseled patience while Jake urged him to make his feelings clearer. Stuck somewhere between the two extremes, Isaac tried to find balance.

It seemed only fair to share some details of his work with Daniella, particularly since she'd been directly involved in the past and he wanted her to understand how vital his job was.

They were sitting together on the porch swing, slowly rocking, when he decided to bring up Leon Ridge. "Looks like we were right about Harland Jeffries being dirty." Isaac was leaning forward, elbows resting on his knees, fingers clasped between them. "Leon's started talking."

"Was he an eyewitness to the shootings at the estate?"

"Not exactly. He claims the congressman called him in a panic, though," Isaac told her.

"That's something. Maybe we won't have to bother poor, scared little Tommy again."

"Probably not. Apparently, the boy didn't see much more than what he's already told us. Nobody did. Two men were yelling at each other and the white-haired one had a gun. That's about it."

Isaac straightened and slipped an arm over the back of the swing, ready to lay it across her shoulders if she seemed agreeable, particularly since she wasn't wearing the sling.

"So, what did happen?" Daniella asked.

"If you can believe Leon, Jeffries insisted he hadn't meant to hurt Michael. They'd been arguing about taking proper care of Juan, the little boy with the birthmark in the photo we saw at the foster care safe house. Michael was supposedly threatening to go public about his father's affair with Rosa Gomez and Juan's birth, for the sake of the child's future. They struggled. The gun went off and Michael was wounded."

"Why didn't anybody call for help?"

Isaac shrugged. "Good question. Maybe Michael died too quickly. We can't be sure. Anyway, Harland phoned Leon and together they figured out an alibi. Leon swears he was only supposed to lightly wound the congressman so Harland could claim the same assailant was responsible for killing Michael. He almost overdid it, though. Harland passed out before he could call 911 and could have died before he regained consciousness."

"But—" Daniella was frowning and slowly shaking her head "—where does my father fit in all of this? He wasn't working for Jeffries, was he?"

"No, not according to Leon, and everything we've been able to substantiate so far has proved true. It looks as if Harland was so mentally unbalanced after shooting Michael he wasn't thinking straight. When I recently interviewed him about the bomb that went off during his press conference, he figured I knew he was responsible, which was correct. Unfortunately, to his twisted mind, my visit to his office also meant I knew more about his other crimes than I actually did, including the death of his son. Leon says the guy was convinced that getting rid of me and blaming it on Fagan was the answer to all his problems."

"That's crazy."

"Uh-huh. Very. I had already reported most of what I knew. Besides, you and Cassie both heard Tommy ID the congressman as the armed man, so logically, you two should have been on his hit list, too." He paused, thinking about all that had taken place and how blessed they were to still have each other.

"So, what now?"

"Captain McCord has requested a search warrant for the Jeffries estate and the congressman's office. We're planning to raid both at the same time."

"When?"

Isaac checked his watch, then replaced his arm behind her shoulders and pulled her closer. He sighed deeply when she snuggled against him. "In a few hours. We'll wait until dark to minimize the danger to bystanders."

"Surely Harland won't be in his office then."

"We hope not. We'd like to confine the risk to his estate."

"And to yourselves," Daniella added as she laid her palm on his chest. "I wish you didn't have to be involved."

"You mean you wish I had a different job?"

Leaning away slightly, she studied his face for a few moments before starting to smile. "No. I can see you're doing exactly what you were meant to do. It's Jeffries who worries me. If he's as mentally unbalanced as you say he is, how can you be sure you won't be greeted by a hail of bullets?"

"Like I've said before, Gavin—my captain—has been close to Harland ever since he was a teenage resident of the foster home on the Jeffries estate. He'll go in first and make sure the congressman is unarmed, if he's home."

"This must be really hard on your captain."

"It is." Isaac clenched his jaw as he considered that truth.

"Um, speaking of hard jobs, I want you to hurry home. There's something I'd like to talk about."

"So, talk." He glanced at his watch again. "I've got a few minutes to spare."

"Oh, no, you don't." She shook her head so hard her silky hair swung back and forth over her shoulders. "I've seen you use your job as an excuse to run off in the middle of an important conversation, and I'm not taking any chances."

"You're serious?"

"Totally."

Isaac leaned closer and used one finger to tilt up her chin before giving her a tender kiss. "In that case, here's a little something for you to think about while I'm gone."

Abby was part of the assault team that entered the Jeffries mansion on McCord's signal. Other officers raided the congressman's DC office at the same time.

Gavin McCord was standing in the center of the ornately furnished living room and holding a small black book when Isaac and Abby approached him.

"I want you to check the whole house for any trace of explosives," McCord ordered. "I don't think you'll turn up anything like that, but it never hurts to play it safe."

"What about Harland? Did you find him?"

"No. The few servants he has left swear they haven't seen him since breakfast."

"Do you believe them?"

McCord nodded, disgust and disappointment evident. "I suppose the political grapevine warned him somehow. I should have anticipated that."

"Well, at least his focus is off Washington. He has to know his political career is finished. Where do you think he went?"

"Probably overseas, wherever he's stashed a getaway fund." The captain waved the notebook. "It looks like it's all in here, the bribes, the deals under the table, the coconspirators. He even orchestrated the plot to steal George Washington's golden arrow from the American

Museum a few months back. I've already ordered the arrest of his other aides."

"All of them were crooks?"

"No. He apparently kept a few on payroll who were
squeaky-clean, probably in case he needed an alibi or a
handy scapegoat. We'll sort them out."

"Where did you find a book like that? I can't believe
he'd be careless enough to leave it lying around."

"He didn't. It was hidden in his safe room, the last
place I checked when nobody could locate him." McCord
started off and motioned Isaac to follow with Abby. "You
can start in there, then work the rest of the house with the
team while I coordinate with Fiona and our other techs
to search his personal online records."

"What about Erin Eagleton? Did Ridge exonerate
her?"

"No." McCord stared at Isaac before pulling out a cell
phone and punching a number, then holding up a hand
to signal Isaac to wait.

"Fiona," he barked, "get me everything Jeffries had
in his records that has anything to do with Senator Eagleton or his daughter, Erin, I don't care how obscure."

Isaac could hear her forceful, enthusiastic "Yes, sir"
and that made him smile. If anybody could dig out the
truth, it was Fiona. For all her quirks, she was the best
computer tech in the business, although she'd had more
than a few moments of inattentiveness since she'd fallen
for one of their secondary K-9 officers, Chris Torrance.

Remembering how clues had pointed to Erin being on
the scene when Michael was shot and how the congressman had implied that she must have pulled the trigger,
Isaac was worried. Judging by the expression on the captain's face, he was, too. Without the murder gun to check

for a ballistic match or fingerprints, placing blame was anybody's guess.

Was Jeffries thinking of his own escape at this time or had he disappeared because was he bent on finding and harming Erin so she couldn't refute his claims?

Only time would tell. Isaac just hoped nobody else had to pay for the crooked congressman's sins.

The body count was already far too high.

Daniella was sitting on the front porch, wearing a quilt like a shawl and waiting for Isaac, when he finally got home.

Parking, he let Abby loose and plodded wearily up the steps. "Do you know what time it is?" he asked.

"Yes. It's after two a.m. If you'd let me come with you we could have had our little talk on the drive home."

"Can't it wait until morning? I'm beat."

She laughed lightly. "It is morning."

"So it is. Okay. Got room for me on that swing?"

"I'll make room." She patted the slatted bench next to her. "This shouldn't take long, unless you make the mistake of arguing with me."

"You know I'd never do that." He was sending a look at her that was half scowl, half smile. "You're not getting up the courage to tell me you've changed your mind *again* and are leaving, are you?"

"Don't bother putting on that hurt expression. You won't need it. I'm not going anywhere. I'm just nervous."

"Why should you be afraid? Your sworn enemy is dead, Leon Ridge is in jail, there's a warrant out for Jeffries and the case against him is coming together. We'll have him in no time."

"I'm not concerned about criminals. Your unit and

the other cops can worry about them. From now on I'm staying out of it."

"So…?"

She laid her fingertips over his lips, ostensibly to silence him, and he kissed them instead.

"Stop distracting me."

"Why? You keep distracting me."

Daniella blew a noisy sigh. "I want to talk about the future—our future."

"Ours?"

She laughed again, her cheeks blooming in the dimness of the single porch light. "You shouldn't be surprised. I've done everything I can think of except come right out and ask you if you love me."

"Of course I love you!" Watching tears glimmering in her emerald eyes, Isaac couldn't decide whether to kiss her into silence or let her keep talking.

He was about to choose the kiss when Daniella began to whisk away sparse tears.

"Okay," she said, sniffling and smiling. "So when are you going to tell me what you plan to do about it?"

"What do *you* want to do?"

"Uh-uh. No fair. If I have to tell you that I want you to sweep me off my feet and ask me to marry you, it won't be as romantic."

Stunned by both her boldness and the way her ideas had meshed so perfectly with his, Isaac laughed. "Suppose I surprise you one day soon with a ring? Will that do?"

"It might, if you don't wait too long."

"I'll do my best," he said, sobering. "I'll always do my best for you, honey. You know that, don't you?"

She reached up and cupped his cheek.

Isaac placed his hand over hers, then drew it down to kiss her palm. There would never be a dull day married to this extraordinary woman, he realized, counting his blessings again and again. And he would guard his life for her sake as well as his own.

"I think your sister was right when she said the Lord brought us together," Daniella whispered. "So it's a good thing we fell in love. I sure wouldn't want to disappoint God after He went to all that trouble."

Isaac gave her a heartfelt kiss. "I agree. Prepare to say yes when I pop the question."

He saw her lips tremble, her eyes glisten, as she smiled and said, "I can hardly wait."

* * * * *

If you liked this CAPITOL K-9 UNIT *novel,*
watch for the next book in the series,
PROOF OF INNOCENCE by Lenora Worth

And don't miss a single story in the
CAPITOL K-9 UNIT *miniseries:*

Book #1: PROTECTION DETAIL
by Shirlee McCoy

Book #2: DUTY BOUND GUARDIAN
by Terri Reed

Book #3: TRAIL OF EVIDENCE
by Lynette Eason

Book #4: SECURITY BREACH
by Margaret Daley

Book #5: DETECTING DANGER
by Valerie Hansen

Book #6: PROOF OF INNOCENCE
by Lenora Worth

Dear Reader,

As you can see, I'm involved in yet another continuity series. These are organized by my publisher, which then invites various authors to participate. The more of these I write, the more friends I make and the more I appreciate how difficult it can be to tell an ongoing story while still keeping some secrets for the final book.

Real life can seem like that sometimes. We can't see the whole picture, so we suffer, worry and doubt God. The longer I live, the more I can look back and see the Lord's hand in situations that were beyond my understanding at the time they occurred. And I still have questions. Without my Christian faith, however, I know I would not be able to cope, and I urge you to place your trust in God, too. You won't be sorry.

Thanks to my fellow authors, Shirlee McCoy, Terri Reed, Lynette Eason, Margaret Daley and Lenora Worth. It's been a pleasure, as always.

Blessings,

Valerie Hansen

REQUEST YOUR FREE BOOKS!
2 FREE RIVETING INSPIRATIONAL NOVELS
PLUS 2 FREE MYSTERY GIFTS

Love Inspired®
SUSPENSE
RIVETING INSPIRATIONAL ROMANCE

YES! Please send me 2 FREE Love Inspired® Suspense novels and my 2 FREE mystery gifts (gifts are worth about $10). After receiving them, if I don't wish to receive any more books, I can return the shipping statement marked "cancel." If I don't cancel, I will receive 4 brand-new novels every month and be billed just $4.99 per book in the U.S. or $5.49 per book in Canada. That's a savings of at least 17% off the cover price. It's quite a bargain! Shipping and handling is just 50¢ per book in the U.S. and 75¢ per book in Canada.* I understand that accepting the 2 free books and gifts places me under no obligation to buy anything. I can always return a shipment and cancel at any time. Even if I never buy another book, the two free books and gifts are mine to keep forever.

123/323 IDN GH5Z

Name	(PLEASE PRINT)	

Address		Apt. #

City	State/Prov.	Zip/Postal Code

Signature (if under 18, a parent or guardian must sign)

Mail to the **Reader Service:**
IN U.S.A.: P.O. Box 1867, Buffalo, NY 14240-1867
IN CANADA: P.O. Box 609, Fort Erie, Ontario L2A 5X3

**Are you a current subscriber to Love Inspired® Suspense books
and want to receive the larger-print edition?
Call 1-800-873-8635 or visit www.ReaderService.com.**

* Terms and prices subject to change without notice. Prices do not include applicable taxes. Sales tax applicable in N.Y. Canadian residents will be charged applicable taxes. Offer not valid in Quebec. This offer is limited to one order per household. Not valid for current subscribers to Love Inspired Suspense books. All orders subject to credit approval. Credit or debit balances in a customer's account(s) may be offset by any other outstanding balance owed by or to the customer. Please allow 4 to 6 weeks for delivery. Offer available while quantities last.

Your Privacy—The Reader Service is committed to protecting your privacy. Our Privacy Policy is available online at www.ReaderService.com or upon request from the Reader Service.
We make a portion of our mailing list available to reputable third parties that offer products we believe may interest you. If you prefer that we not exchange your name with third parties, or if you wish to clarify or modify your communication preferences, please visit us at www.ReaderService.com/consumerschoice or write to us at Reader Service Preference Service, P.O. Box 9062, Buffalo, NY 14240-9062. Include your complete name and address.

LIS15

*Can the Capitol K-9 Unit find Erin Eagleton and solve
the mystery of her boyfriend's death before it's too late?*

*Read on for a sneak preview of
PROOF OF INNOCENCE,
the conclusion to the exciting saga
CAPITOL K-9 UNIT.*

An urgent heartbeat pounded through Erin Eagleton's
temples each time her feet hit the dry, packed earth. She
stumbled, grabbed at a leafy sapling and checked behind
her again. The tree's slender limbs hit at her face and neck
when she let go, leaving red welts across her cheekbones,
but she kept running. Soon it would be full dark, and she
would have to find a safe place to hide.

Winded and damp with a cold sweat that shivered
down her backbone, Erin tried to catch her breath. Did
she dare stop and try to find another path?

The sound of approaching footsteps behind her caused
Erin to take off to the right and head deeper into the
woods. She had to keep running. But she was so tired.
Would she ever be free?

Memories of Chase Zachary moved through her head,
causing tears to prick at her eyes. Her first love. Her high
school sweetheart who now worked as a K-9 officer with
an elite Washington, DC, team. A team that was investigating her.

From what she'd read on the internet and in the local papers, Chase had been one of the first officers on the scene that horrible night.

She'd thought about calling him a hundred times over these past few months, but Erin wasn't sure she could trust even Chase. The last time they'd seen each other last winter, on the very evening this nightmare had taken place, he hadn't been very friendly. He probably hated her for breaking his heart when they were so young.

But then just about everybody else along the beltway hated her right now. Erin had been on the run for months. She knew running made her look guilty, but she'd had no other choice since she'd witnessed the murder of her boyfriend, Michael Jeffries, and she'd almost been killed herself. The authorities thought she was the killer and until she could prove otherwise, Erin had to stay hidden.

Don't miss
PROOF OF INNOCENCE
by Lenora Worth,
available August 2015 wherever
Love Inspired® Suspense books and ebooks are sold.

"So you'll be wrangling here," Tessa blurted out.

"Yep." His gaze narrowed even more.

Well, that was helpful. Tessa tried again.

"You've been discharged from the navy?"

He frowned and jammed his fists into the front pockets of his worn blue jeans. "Yep."

She was beyond frustrated at his cold reception, but she supposed she had it coming. She could hardly expect better when the last time they'd seen each other was—

Well, there was no use dwelling on the past. If Cole was going to work here with her, he would have to get over it.

So, for that matter, would she.

"Well, I won't keep you," she said, reaching back to open the office door. "I just wanted to make sure we had an understanding about how our professional relationship here at the ranch was going to go."

He scowled at the word *relationship*. "Just came as a surprise, is all," he muttered.

"I'll say," Tessa agreed.

"Didn't expect to be back in Serendipity for a few years yet. Maybe ever."

He sounded so bitter that Tessa cringed. What had happened to the boy she'd once known? Who or what had darkened the sunshine that had once shone so brilliantly in his eyes?

"Cole? Why did you come back now?"

He tipped his hat and started to walk past her without speaking, and Tessa thought she'd pushed him too far. Whatever his issues were, clearly she was the last person on earth he'd talk to about them.

He was almost out the door when he suddenly swiveled around to face her.

"Grayson." His gaze narrowed on her as if weighing the effect of his words on her.

She scrambled to put his answer in some kind of context but came up with nothing.

"Who—"

He cut off her question and ground out the rest of his answer.

"My son."

Don't miss
THE COWBOY'S SURPRISE BABY by Deb Kastner,
available August 2015 wherever
Love Inspired® books and ebooks are sold.

LIEXP0715